He leaned close and whispered in her ear, "If someone is watching you, you need to convince them I'm not a threat."

She frowned up at him. "And how do you intend to do that?" she asked, matching his low tones.

He nuzzled her neck and breathed into her ear, "They need to think I'm supposed to be with you."

She tipped her head back and closed her eyes, all the while keeping her voice down. "They know I don't have any other siblings, and I've never known any cousins."

"What about a boyfriend?" Mack suggested, running his hand up beneath her hair. "Are you known to have a boyfriend or lover?"

Butterflies erupted in Riley's belly at the touch of his hand on the back of her neck. "No. I haven't had time to cultivate a romance. I've been too busy living two lives to add another to the mix."

He leaned back and smiled down into her eyes. "Then let's set the stage for anyone watching."

"What do you mean?" She stiffened, her insides trembling, her body warming with excitement.

"Meet your new boyfriend."

SHOW OF FORCE

New York Times Bestselling Author

ELLE JAMES

DISCARD

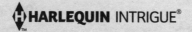
HARLEQUIN INTRIGUE®

This book is dedicated to my mother, who has always been there for me, my sister and brothers. When my father was deployed to other parts of the world, she was the one who held down the fort at home. She's beautiful, talented and determined. She encouraged us to follow our own paths, wherever they might lead.

I love you, Mom!

ISBN-13: 978-1-335-60433-0

Show of Force

Copyright © 2019 by Mary Jernigan

Recycling programs for this product may not exist in your area.

Printed in U.S.A.

HARLEQUIN®
™ www.Harlequin.com

A12007 273695

Elle James, a *New York Times* bestselling author, started writing when her sister challenged her to write a romance novel. She has managed a full-time job and raised three wonderful children, and she and her husband even tried ranching exotic birds (ostriches, emus and rheas). Ask her, and she'll tell you what it's like to go toe-to-toe with an angry 350-pound bird! Elle loves to hear from fans at ellejames@earthlink.net or ellejames.com.

Books by Elle James

Harlequin Intrigue

Declan's Defenders

Mission: Six

Ballistic Cowboys

SEAL of My Own

Visit the Author Profile page at Harlequin.com.

CAST OF CHARACTERS

Mack Balkman—Former Force Recon marine, assistant team leader, Declan's right-hand man. Grew up on a farm and knows hard work won't kill you. Guns will.

Riley Lansing—Engineer on special projects at Quest Aerospace Alliance. Born in the US to Russian parents, she was secretly trained as a Russian sleeper agent.

Declan O'Neill—Highly trained Force Recon marine who made a decision that cost him his career in the Marine Corps. After being dishonorably discharged from the military, he's forging his own path with the help of a wealthy benefactor.

Charlotte "Charlie" Halverson—Rich widow of a highly prominent billionaire philanthropist. Leading the fight for right by funding Declan's Defenders.

Frank "Mustang" Ford—Former Force Recon marine, point man. First into dangerous situations, making him the eyes and ears of the team.

Augustus "Gus" Walsh—Former Force Recon marine radio operator, good with weapons, electronics and technical equipment.

Cole McCastlain—Former Force Recon marine assistant radio operator. Good with computers.

Jack Snow—Former Force Recon marine slack man, youngest on the team, takes all the heavy stuff. Not afraid of hard, physical work.

Margaret Weems—Riley's old friend and her brother's nanny.

Bryan Young—Head of Riley's department at Quest Aerospace Alliance.

Steve Pruett—Project engineer on special projects. Riley's private coworker.

Tracy Gibson—Secretary to Riley's former supervisor.

Brigett Paulson—Member of the janitorial service at Quest Aerospace Alliance.

Chapter One

Just after four o'clock in the afternoon, Riley Lansing slipped in through the back entrance of the Marriott Marquis hotel in downtown Washington, DC. She wore a stolen employee badge and one of the dresses required of the female waitstaff. With her dark hair tucked beneath a blond wig, she passed for the woman in the fuzzy image sufficiently enough to make it past the security guard.

She carried a large purse and smacked chewing gum. When the guard asked to search her bag, she made certain her less-than-sexy panties and feminine products were on top to discourage him from digging deeper and discovering her second costume of the night.

Her trick worked. The guard waved her past the checkpoint.

Riley sailed through and entered the employee

locker room. Instead of ditching her bag, she carried it through to the door on the far side that led deeper into the hotel's service area.

Riley's heart pounded against her ears, and her pulse thundered through her veins. She'd trained most of her young life for this. Her mother and father had drilled her daily on her responsibilities and loyalties. But Riley had hoped and prayed she would be forgotten, shuffled into the far regions of some paper file that had never been converted to digital data.

All the years she'd immersed herself in the American life her parents had created for her, with their own false identities and her legitimate birth certificate, were about to be blown wide open. No one she'd come into contact with over her lifetime knew her as anyone but Riley Lansing, daughter of Linda and Robert Lansing. Her parents spoke perfect American English and appeared to be the finest of upstanding citizens of the good old US of A.

Only they weren't. She wasn't. Her life had been one big lie, leading up to what she'd been tasked to do that evening.

Why now? Why, after the deaths of her father and mother in an auto accident five years earlier, had they come back to call her to service? Riley had hoped her parents' handler had forgotten their daughter and her little brother even existed.

She'd pushed her secret life to the back of her consciousness for so long, she almost believed it was all a weird dream made up from a child's wild imagination.

Until that morning, when she'd received the electronically distorted message from an anonymous voice initiating her call to action. "Baryshnikov has risen."

At first, she hadn't recognized the code words. When they sank in from the years her father had repeated them, a chill raised the hairs on the back of her neck and rippled down the length of her spine.

"You will find instructions at the luggage storage area at the Metro in downtown DC." The voice left an address and locker number. "And to guarantee your compliance, we have a little insurance policy."

A moment later, little Toby's voice came through the receiver. "Riley?" he said, the one word catching on a sob. "I'm scared."

"Oh, Toby. Sweetheart," she said. "It's okay. I'm coming for you. I'll find you and bring you home."

Her little brother sobbed once more, jerking at Riley's heartstrings.

"Toby?" Riley cried out.

"Do the job tonight and the boy will be returned to his home," the voice said. "Fail and you will never see him again."

Clutching the large bag close to her side, she hurried through the maze of corridors she'd traversed the day before, familiarizing herself with the layout of the kitchen, the staff elevators and the ballroom where the evening's event would take place. She'd even identified an electronics closet where she could hide until the event began, ensuring she'd be past the security guards who would be posted at every entrance and exit checking identification against invitation lists.

The second worst part of her plan was the two hours she'd have to wait until she could initiate the operation.

The absolute worst part of her plan was the crux of the operation and what she had to accomplish to satisfy her handler and get her little brother back alive.

To succeed at her mission, she had to kill someone she not only knew but admired.

Her hand shook as she slipped a file into the keyhole and jimmied the lock on the door to the electronics closet. It clicked, and she pulled the door open. She'd played with locks from an early age and could open just about anything requiring a key. This skill had come in handy during college when she entered her dorm past curfew and the doors were locked.

Once inside the electronics room, she closed the door and locked it from the inside to keep anyone from randomly walking in looking for something or someone.

For the next two and a half hours, she waited.

The security detail would have swept the ballroom and surrounding cubbies, restrooms, hallways and anterooms. Guards would have been positioned at all corners, equipped with radio communications devices and handguns.

Her target would have no fewer than four bodyguards in attendance. Having had an attempt made on her life recently, she wouldn't take any chances. Not even at a gala with the prime purpose of raising money for sick children.

During the two hours Riley waited, she went through her proposed actions in her mind, the steps she would take and how she would maneuver her victim out of the ballroom and into one of the anterooms or the ladies' restroom. Once there, Riley would aim her small handgun at the woman and force her to take a small pill. She slipped her hand into the voluminous purse and curled her fingers around the HK .40 caliber handgun that fit snugly in her grip. She knew how to fire it. Knew where to hit her target to ensure a quick and painless death. But she wouldn't fire the handgun unless absolutely necessary. The poison would do the trick much more quietly. All she had to do was make her take it, and Toby would be set free.

She couldn't think about the woman she'd been sent to eliminate. Toby was only six years old. He deserved a chance to live. If it meant taking the life of an older woman who'd had her chance at living, so be it. Riley couldn't let anything happen to her only living relative remaining on earth. As far as she knew, Toby didn't know what her parents and she herself had been recruited to do.

No one knew, except Riley and her handler. And Riley had no clue who her handler was. When her parents died, she'd taken on guardianship of her little brother. She should have known hiding him in the Virginia countryside with a paid nanny wouldn't be enough to keep him safe. When her parents had passed away, she should have moved as far away from DC as she could get. At least then the Russians wouldn't have been able to find Toby and use him as collateral to collect on their investment.

As the time neared, her breathing became more erratic and her pulse raced. In less than an hour, she'd have to put her skills as an assassin to use on an innocent woman who had gone out of her way, spent her money and engaged her employees to help Riley. She'd betray the woman's trust and the trust of her new assistant, Riley's best friend and roommate, Grace Lawrence.

Riley swallowed hard on the bile rising up her throat. She'd never asked for this assignment. She'd spent her life training with the misguided belief she'd never have to use that training. If asked to do something she didn't like, she'd always imagined herself refusing.

Until they'd kidnapped Toby. Toby was her Achilles' heel. She'd do anything for her little brother.

Even kill?

The alarm on her watch vibrated, letting her know the time had come. She had to get ready and make an appearance at the gala. Her target would recognize her and welcome her with open arms. She might even wonder how Riley could have afforded the plate price to get in. Riley had a lame excuse to cover long enough to get her quarry alone. She'd take her someplace where she could be assured they wouldn't be followed by the woman's bodyguards. There, she would do what she'd come to do.

Riley removed the blond wig, slipped the maid's dress over her head, released the clasps on her bra and slid the straps down her arms. Naked but for a pair of silky black panties, she wrapped a small amount of C-4 explosive to her inner calf with an Ace bandage and tucked the detonator affixed to a hair clip into her long dark hair, pulling it back behind her right ear and letting the rest of her hair fall over her left shoulder. The C-4 and detonator were courtesy of her handler, from among the items she'd found in the locker he'd sent her to in the train station.

Once she had her diversion devices secured, she dug a long black dress out of the bottom lining of her purse and shook out the wrinkles. She'd purchased the dress while shopping with her friend, intending to wear it to a less expensive charity event later that summer.

She almost laughed at the thought. That was when she was still an innocent American female who had nothing more to worry about than riding the Metro to and from her work as an aerospace engineer. The irony of it all was that she'd been recruited by the FBI to help them capture someone stealing government secrets from the corporation where she worked.

They'd come close but hadn't nailed the bastard. What was so ironic was that thief might have been working for the Russians. Just like she was.

She pulled the dress over her head, settling the halter strap around her neck and letting the silky gown slide down her torso and over her hips. Riley and her roommate had both loved the dress. Though it had been a little pricey for her budget, she'd purchased the garment, excited to wear it to a ritzy DC function.

She no longer was the child easily molded and trained by her parents. That little girl had grown into a woman with a mind of her own. All the propaganda her parents had used to shape her beliefs had been replaced by the readings and research of an inquisitive mind. She had no desire to work as a spy or an assassin for a country for which she felt no affiliation. She was an American, despite her parents' home of birth. She wanted the American dream, the American lifestyle, and the right to pursue happiness and love. And she'd hoped to accomplish some of that pursuit in the dress she'd purchased with her roommate.

Riley tucked the murder weapon into the bra of her dress. A tiny plastic bag containing one small pill that only had to touch the victim's tongue to do the job. The pill would dissolve before anyone could do anything to help her, and the damage would be done. She'd die within just two minutes, her body hemorrhaging internally.

Pulling a small mirror from her purse, she examined her makeup and the dress in an entirely different light from that of the happy young professional engineer she'd been when she purchased the item. In that dress, her life would change forever.

To Riley, the dress would always be what she'd worn when she committed murder.

"ARE WE HERE?" Charlotte Halverson asked as the limousine pulled up to the curb outside the Marriott Marquis hotel in downtown Washington, DC.

Mack Balkman had the lead on the bodyguard detail for his new boss. "Yes, ma'am."

"And don't call me ma'am," the woman said. "It's Charlie."

"Yes, ma'am—Charlie." Mack choked on calling his new boss by her first name. His years on active duty made him want to address his boss with the utmost respect. And if that wasn't bad enough, his parents had insisted he address women older than him by their surnames. Calling Mrs. Halverson by her first name didn't sit right in his books. But she was the boss, and if she wanted him to call her Pookie while standing on his head, he'd do it. She'd given him a job when most others wouldn't have given him the time of day.

"Are my men in place?" Charlie asked.

"They are. We've got you covered." He touched his headset. "All clear?"

Mustang, their point man who'd arrived on a motorcycle ahead of them, replied, "Ready as we can be. This place is crawling with people here to see the red-carpet show."

Augustus "Gus" Walsh climbed out of the passenger seat of the limousine and opened the back door.

When Charlie started to slide across the seat, Mack touched her arm. "Normally, I'd say ladies first, but not tonight."

"Right." Charlie settled back and waited for Mack to exit the vehicle.

He stood, straightened the tuxedo she'd arranged for him to wear and patted the nine-millimeter SIG Sauer P226 tucked beneath his jacket. Under his white shirt and cummerbund, he wore a bulletproof vest. He'd already cleared his men through the service that had been hired to provide security for the annual gala. All they had to do was show their identification and they would bypass the metal detectors that would make all kinds of noise if they found guns or knives on those who passed through.

He held out his hand for Charlie and helped the older woman from the back of the limousine. Gus closed ranks, moving in on the other side of her. He used his body as a shield against any potential threat.

They couldn't be too careful. Less than two weeks prior, an attempt had been made on Charlie's life. Two vans full of bad guys had cornered her limousine on a busy DC street. They'd killed her previous bodyguards and attempted a kidnapping. Thankfully, former Force Recon marine Declan O'Neill, Mack's old team leader, had been there to save her. She'd rewarded him by hiring him and his team to provide security for her or anyone she deemed in need of assistance.

"You gentlemen don't know how safe it makes me feel to have highly qualified, loyal men protecting me." Charlie patted his arm. "I can't tell you how happy I am that Declan agreed to come on board and bring his team with him."

"Ma'am—" Mack started.

"Charlie," she said.

Gus smiled. "I don't know about you, Mack, but I have a hard time calling her Charlie myself. She could be my mo—"

Charlie held up her hand. "Don't say it."

Gus clamped his lips shut.

Mack hid a smile.

"Don't say I'm old enough to be your mother. I feel old enough as it is. But my mind is still sharp and I feel like a twenty-five-year-old, thanks to Edwardo, my personal trainer." She lifted her chin. "And this dress makes me feel like a million bucks." She sighed. "My husband would have liked me in it."

"You look amazing, Charlie," Mack said. "But I'd feel better if you looked amazing inside the hotel. Not out here on the streets where anything can happen."

"Right." Charlie forced a smile to her lips and stepped out on Mack's arm.

He knew he appeared to be more a date than a bodyguard, but he didn't care, as long as he had room under his jacket for a weapon. He scanned the crowds of people standing on the other side of a barricade. Photographers snapped pictures and bystanders watched as vehicles pulled up one by one, discharging well-dressed men and women onto the red carpet.

Mack and Gus eased their charge along.

Charlie smiled and waved at the reporters and the people like a celebrity on a walk of fame.

From what Declan had told Mack and the other men of his team, Declan's Defenders, Mrs. Charlotte Halverson was a kind of celebrity in her own right. The rich widow of a prominent philanthropist, she'd rubbed elbows with some of the most influential people of the century, from Hollywood movie stars to the leaders of many countries, including the president of the United States.

Charlie stopped and waited her turn to have her official photograph taken in front of the gala's backdrop. Ahead of her was a younger couple, the woman wearing a fancy silver gown with sequins and a diamond necklace that probably cost more than what Mack had made in a year as a marine.

He didn't envy the woman her jewelry or the money it took to buy it. Instead, he cringed at the amount of money wasted on jewelry that could be given to the charity the gala was raising money for.

But he wasn't there to judge the people attending; he was employed to keep Charlie safe.

When it was Charlie's turn to have her picture taken, she insisted on Mack standing with her.

"Wouldn't you rather have one of your friends pose with you?" Mack asked.

"These people are acquaintances. Besides, you're much better-looking than they are. I'd love to make them all jealous." She smiled up at him. "But if it makes you uncomfortable, you don't have to be in the picture."

"I'd prefer to stay close," he said.

"Good. Then it's settled." She led him to stand in front of the backdrop. Once they were there, photographers snapped their pictures.

The flashes temporarily blinded Mack. He touched a finger to his headset. "Keep your eyes peeled," he said softly.

"No worries," Gus responded. "We've got Charlie covered while you're playing the model."

Mustang chuckled. "Nice tux. Didn't know you could clean up so well."

"Damned monkey suit," Mack muttered.

"I heard that," Charlie said between her teeth as she smiled for the camera.

"Sorry."

"Don't worry. My husband hated to dress up as well. But the gala for the children was one of his favorites. He wouldn't miss it for the world." Her smile faded. "He would have loved being here."

Mack realized he didn't know much about the Halversons, other than what had been printed in the tabloids. He wondered how long they were married and whether they'd had children.

"You see, my husband and I weren't blessed with children." She hooked her arm through his and left the photographers' circle and continued on toward the hotel. "We tried, but it wasn't meant to be. All the money we would have spent raising and educating one of our own went into scholarships, research and a new wing on the children's hospital. My husband didn't live to see the wing complete."

"Did they capture your husband's killer?" Mack asked.

Charlie shook her head. "No. And that's part of the reason why I decided to hire your team leader. The police force is too overwhelmed with work to find all the bad guys. I figured I could help, if only just a little."

They entered the building and moved with the flow of people toward the main ballroom.

The crush of guests all dressed in glitz and glamour surrounded Mack and Charlie. Mack's first instinct was to grab Charlie and back away. How would he keep her safe in a room as crowded as it was?

He gripped her elbow and slowed her to a halt.

Charlie frowned. "What's wrong?"

"There are far too many people in this room," he said.

Her frown easily turned into a smile. "The more the merrier. The charity will get lots of donations."

Mack grunted. "I'm more worried about your safety. You need to hang out on the fringes where we can give you better coverage."

"Oh, pooh." Her smile slipped. "And my safety

isn't as important as getting the money needed for the research that could provide cures for children with life-threatening diseases. My husband was a big proponent of this particular aid group. I won't hide behind my bodyguard when there are children in need of cures." She shook her arm loose of Mack's grip and marched into the middle of the ballroom, smiling like a Valkyrie declaring victory.

"What's wrong?" Gus asked. "Why is Charlie alone in the middle of the room?"

"I think it was easier facing the Taliban than working for Mrs. Halverson," Mack muttered. "The woman has a mind of her own, and she doesn't like following orders."

"I'm not liking it," Mustang said into Mack's ear. "We can't protect her if she's not willing to protect herself."

"You're telling me," Mack said, and pushed his way through the throngs of elegantly dressed people until he arrived at Charlie's side.

"Well, darn," she said, and smiled up at Mack, the lines at the corners of her eyes crinkling with mischief. "I thought I'd lost you."

"Please, Mrs. H—"

She raised a finger. "Uh-uh."

Mack sighed. "Charlie, don't go running off. I can't protect you if I'm not at your side."

"I want you to keep me safe, but I can't take you everywhere."

Mack straightened to his full six foot three inches. "Where you go, I go."

Charlie raised her brows. "I'm sorry?"

"If you want my protection, you have to follow my rules."

Charlie crossed her arms over her chest and raised her salt-and-pepper brows. "Not to the ladies' room, I should think."

Mack frowned deeply. He hadn't thought about areas off-limits to men. Perhaps they should have hired a female bodyguard just for that purpose. For now, he'd have to make do. "I'll clear the room before you go in."

Charlie patted Mack's cheek and smiled. "Sweetie, that won't be necessary. I can manage a trip to the restroom on my own."

If he was going to do the job right, he had to know exactly where his charge was at all times. Disappearing behind a closed door was not something Charlie could do without having him or one of his men check the facilities first. He'd cross that bridge when they came to it. For the moment, he kept busy chasing the wealthy widow around the ballroom.

An hour into the night's festivities, Charlie exclaimed, "Oh, look who's here."

Mack glanced in the direction Charlie was looking.

A dark-haired woman in a long black dress stood next to a man in a white tuxedo. She nodded, spoke to the man, made him laugh and then looked up. A moment later, she was walking toward Charlie, a smile spreading across her face. "Mrs. Halverson, I didn't know you'd be here."

"My dear, wild horses couldn't drag me away. This is the one charity event I can't miss." She clasped the woman's hands. "Mack, you remember Riley Lansing, don't you?" Charlie squeezed Riley's hands and let go, then turned to Mack. "She was the woman who led us on quite the wild chase a couple weeks ago. In fact, it was her roommate's concern for her that made me consider spinning up Declan's Defenders."

Mack remembered Riley. "I'm sorry. I barely recognized you."

"That's okay." She smiled. "I guess I clean up well."

Mack couldn't keep his gaze from traversing the length of the black dress from her neck to her toes. The fabric clung to her curves like a second skin.

"I'm so glad to see you," Charlie said. "For two reasons."

Riley raised her eyebrows. "Two reasons? That sounds pretty specific."

Charlie laughed. "You'll understand in a moment. Number one, I'm glad you're okay. For a while there, we didn't know what had happened to you when you went missing. And two, I couldn't convince Mack to allow me to go to the ladies' room on my own. But I'm sure if I go with you, he won't insist on accompanying me." She gave Mack a challenging lift of her brow.

Mack frowned heavily. "I still think you need me to clear the restroom before you go in."

"Fine." Charlie's lips pressed together. "I'll tell everyone to leave so that my big bad bodyguard can inspect each stall." She shot a glance at Riley. "Do you mind coming with me?"

Riley gave Charlie a tight smile. "Not at all."

Mack studied the younger woman. Something wasn't quite right about her response.

Her hands clenched into tight fists, and a slight glow of perspiration coated her fair skin.

"Miss Lansing, are you feeling well?" he asked.

She jerked her head around to stare up at him. "Yes. Why do you ask?"

He shrugged. "You seem nervous." He tipped his chin toward her balled fists.

She laughed, uncurled her fingers and pressed her palms together. "No. I'm not nervous," she said quickly. And then sighed. "Well, maybe just a little. I don't normally wear fancy clothing or attend expensive galas."

"Speaking of which," Charlotte interrupted, "how

did you manage to get a seat at the event? I thought it had sold out within thirty minutes of going up online."

Riley gave a brief smile. "I won the ticket on a radio talk show."

Mrs. Halverson clapped her hands. "What a gift. This event is one of my favorites. I hope they have the children's choir sing as they have in the past."

"Children's choir?" Riley's eyes widened.

"Yes. They always do. There they are, lining up now." Charlie bit down on her bottom lip. "I'd like to make a trip to the ladies' room before they begin." She reached for Riley's arm. "Do you mind accompanying an old woman? I promise not to make any strange noises." The widow winked and held up her fingers like a Boy Scout. "I swear."

Riley darted a glance at the children lining up near the raised dais where the band had set up earlier. "I suppose I could." She nodded as if making up her mind and turned to take Mrs. Halverson's arm. "Let's get this over with."

Charlie smiled over her shoulder at Mack. "Happy? I have someone looking out for me so you don't have to."

"I'd still like to clear the room before you go in."

"I'll ask people to leave," Riley offered.

Mack informed his other two team members of his intentions and then followed the women to the hallway where the ladies' restroom was located. His gut was tight and roiling just a little. Like the time just before the mission that had ended his marine career. He'd had the same feeling then as he had now.

Charlie waited with Mack outside the restroom while Riley rounded up the occupants and ushered them out. When she returned, she nodded. "The room is clear."

Mack entered, checked each stall and looked for any other doors leading in or out. When he was satisfied no one else was in the room, he returned to Charlie and Riley. "Okay, the room is clear."

"I could have told you that," Riley said. "But I guess you had to see it for yourself."

He nodded and checked his watch. "Five minutes tops. If you're not out by then, I'm coming in."

Charlie smiled. "I can barely get my lipstick out of my purse in five minutes." She patted Mack's arm. "Don't worry. I'll be out by then. If not, please come in and get me. I might be stuck." She laughed all the way through the door.

Riley glanced back as she followed Charlie inside. A frown dented her forehead and gave her a worried look.

Mack opened his mouth to ask what had her concerned, but she disappeared behind the closed door before he uttered a word.

The next five minutes stretched before him like

a chasm. His pulse pounded, and his heart banged against his ribs. Why, he didn't know. He'd checked the room and every stall. No one but Riley was inside the restroom with Charlie. So why was he worried?

Chapter Two

Riley waited for Charlie to enter a stall before she extracted the small plastic packet containing the pill from the bra of her gown. She pulled the clip from her hair and set it on the counter in front of her. Once she administered the poison, she'd set off the small explosion and make her exit in the confusion.

She hadn't counted on Mack being there and so attentive. Her gut clenched, and she closed her eyes, mustering the strength she needed to do what she had to in order to save her brother's life. Toby was only six years old. He deserved the chance to live to a ripe old age. Charlie was in her sixties. She'd lived, loved and traveled the world.

And saved your life by offering the services of Declan's Defenders. She didn't deserve to die any more than Toby. But her death would be much less painful than what her handler would do to Toby if Riley didn't complete the mission.

With her eyes closed, Riley could see Toby's face the last time she'd visited him in the Virginia countryside. He'd been so happy to see her and sad when she'd had to leave. Margaret, the nanny, had smiled and held him like he was her own. The woman was like a grandmother to both Riley and Toby. Riley had known the woman her entire life.

Riley hated leaving but knew she had to go back to her job at Quest Aerospace Alliance that Monday or she'd be missed. Throughout her life, her parents had warned her she would be called on to perform for her mother country one day. The tasks were yet to be determined. She'd assumed spying of some sort. Not assassination, though she'd been trained with a variety of weapons and in both defensive and offensive maneuvers.

Within hours of leaving the country house, Riley was back at her apartment with her roommate, Grace Lawrence. In the middle of the night, she'd received the text. Knowing she couldn't confide in her roommate, she'd kept the text to herself and lain awake the remainder of the night until morning. Then she'd had to act as if nothing were the matter. She'd contacted the nanny, who had just woken up and discovered Toby missing.

Thankfully, Margaret, who'd been her nanny

when she was a little girl, hadn't been harmed in the abduction. But Toby was gone. Explaining to Margaret that she couldn't call the police had been difficult. But she'd calmed Margaret and prayed she'd have the strength to hold off calling the authorities when Riley wanted to do the same.

If she had called the cops, what would she have told them? *Hi, I'm a Russian spy. I don't want to be, but I'm tasked with assassinating a wealthy widow in order to save my brother.*

She'd be locked up faster than she could say *seriously.*

And Toby would be absorbed into the Russian spy machine, tortured and brainwashed until he didn't know right from wrong.

Sweet heaven, she had to go through with the assassination. She couldn't abandon Toby to Russian machinations.

A hand touched her arm, making Riley jump.

"Riley, honey, what's wrong?" Mrs. Halverson stood behind her, wearing a silver gown that complemented her silver hair. The slim woman still appeared beautiful despite the lines and wrinkles on her face. And the frown she wore was soft and worried. About her.

Riley stared into her clear blue eyes for a very long moment, the tiny plastic bag burning her hand.

All she had to do was open it, shove the pill into the older woman's mouth, and it would all be over.

Her hand shook. Trembling started at her knees and rippled all the way up her back. "I can't," she whispered. "I'm so sorry, Toby. I just can't."

The tiny plastic bag dropped from her nerveless fingers and drifted to the floor.

Mrs. Halverson bent to retrieve it.

"No!" Riley tried to grab the bag from the woman, but Charlie held it out of her reach.

"What is this?" the widow asked.

"Nothing. I was just going to flush it down the toilet." She reached for the bag. "Please. Let me have it."

"Is it a drug?" Charlie's gaze captured hers. "Are you taking drugs?"

"No. Of course not," Riley answered automatically.

"Then why do you have it?"

Tears filled Riley's eyes and trickled down her cheeks. "I'm sorry. I'm so sorry."

"For what, my dear?" Charlie pulled Riley into her arms and held her.

"Why did you have to be so nice?" Riley muttered between sobs. "This wouldn't have been so hard if you weren't so good to me."

"What wouldn't be so hard?" Charlie held Riley at arm's length and stared into her eyes. "Tell me what's bothering you. Perhaps I can help."

"Oh, it's no use," Riley shook her head, more tears falling down her face. "The only way you can help is for you to die."

Mrs. Halverson's eyebrows rose on her forehead. "Sweetie, whatever do you mean?"

"The only way to save my brother is for me to assassinate you." Riley nodded toward the plastic bag. "The pill is poison. One touch on your tongue and you'd be dead in seconds."

Charlie's eyes widened, and she held the plastic bag up in front of her. "You wanted to assassinate me? Why? Did I do something to make you mad?"

"Oh, Mrs. Halverson, no. You did everything to help me."

Her forehead wrinkled. "Then why would you want to kill me?"

"They're making me. They have my brother, Toby. If I don't kill you, there's no telling what they'll do to Toby. I'll never see him again. They could kill him, or worse."

"What could be worse?" Mrs. Halverson asked. Then her eyes rounded. "Torture?"

Riley nodded. "And brainwashing. I can't let that happen. He deserves a better life. He's just a child… only six years old."

"Oh dear." Charlie stared at the little bag, shaking her head. "Whatever can you do?"

"Nothing. I can do nothing. My brother will disappear, and I'll never see him again. He'll think I've abandoned him. They'll tell him I never loved him. They'll make him a weapon to use against others in the future." Riley broke away from Mrs. Halverson. "I can't let that happen."

"There's nothing else you can do, then, is there?" the older woman said softly.

Riley stopped pacing and turned to frown at Mrs. Halverson. "What do you mean?"

"You'll have to kill me." The wealthy widow held up the bag. "I'll take the pill and die. Your brother will be safe, and all will end as it should." She started to open the little bag.

Riley dived toward her. "No!" In her effort to stop Mrs. Halverson from doing the dastardly deed, she knocked her to the floor and straddled her.

Mrs. Halverson let out a squeal and grunted as she landed hard on the marble tile.

The door to the restroom burst open. Mack charged in. "What the hell?" He grabbed Riley around the waist and yanked her up off Mrs. Halverson.

"Let go of me!" Riley fought to free herself of Mack's grip, but his iron band of an arm held her tightly against his chest.

"Charlie, are you all right?" Mack asked.

The older woman sat up, still holding the little plastic bag. "I'm okay. Miss Lansing was only helping me to take this pill. It will relieve the headache I'm getting."

"No! Mack, don't let her take that pill. Please, let go of me. She can't take that pill."

"Fiddle. Of course I can." She tilted her head to the side. "It's what you wanted, wasn't it?"

"No," Riley cried. "I never wanted it. Don't do it. Please, don't take that pill." She struggled against the arm holding her around the middle, tearing at Mack's tuxedo sleeve with her fingernails. "Let me go. You don't understand. Please. Don't let her take that pill." Tears poured from her eyes to the point she couldn't see clearly. She blinked rapidly, trying to clear them, trying to see what Mrs. Halverson was doing. Praying she didn't go through with the instructions Riley had been given.

"Mack. Let the dear girl loose." Mrs. Halverson pushed herself to her feet. "I'm quite all right. And for the record, I'm not going to take the pill." She held the packet up. "But we can't just flush it down the toilet. If it's that potent, it could harm someone else."

"What are you talking about?" Mack asked, still holding Riley around her middle. "Is this woman really a threat to you, or not?"

Charlie smiled. "She's not. She just proved she doesn't have it in her to kill."

Riley sobbed. "No, I don't. I've failed Toby. Oh, sweet heaven, I've failed him."

She went limp against Mack, her heart breaking into a million pieces. She'd failed her little brother. What horrible things would happen to him now?

MACK HELD THE woman in the black dress against his chest as she sobbed into his jacket. "Could someone please tell me what's going on?"

"Let me lock the door first." Charlie hurried to the door and twisted the lock, blocking anyone else from accidentally barging in on them.

When she turned to face Mack, she lifted her chin. "We have a situation."

"Do I need to call the others in?" he asked.

Charlie held up a hand. "Not yet. I have a plan on how we can remedy the trouble, but I need your complete cooperation."

"Mine?" Mack shook his head. "I have no idea what you're talking about."

"You will, soon enough." She nodded toward Riley. "Did you know that Miss Lansing was a Russian sleeper spy?"

Mack stared down at the dark head of the woman crying her eyes out into his expensive tuxedo jacket. "Seriously, what's going on? Why is she crying?"

"She's crying because she failed to assassinate me," Charlie said.

Mack shook his head. "Come again?" Had the

woman had too much of the champagne flowing freely throughout the ballroom?

"You heard me." Charlie tipped her head toward the other woman. "Ask Riley."

Touching a thumb beneath Riley's chin, he tipped her wet face upward. The tears on her cheeks made his stomach clench. He wanted to hold her close and chase away whatever was troubling her. "What's Charlie talking about?"

Riley sniffed twice, and then her face crumpled. "She's right. I'm supposed to assassinate her. I'm a Russian sleeper spy, sent to kill Mrs. Charlotte Halverson."

"And if she doesn't, she'll never see her little brother again," Charlie concluded. "I can see no other way to solve this problem but to take the pill she brought to do the deed with and die. Do you?" She tilted her head and stared at Mack.

Mack's jaw dropped. "Are you out of your mind?" He grabbed for the little packet.

Charlie held it out of his grasp. "No, no. Hear me out. In order for Miss Lansing to have time to find her brother and get him out of the clutches of his kidnappers, I have to die."

"Charlie," Mack said in a slow, even tone, though his heart was hammering and his muscles bunched, ready to make another grab for the tiny plastic bag the woman held in her hand. "You didn't hire me to stand by and watch you die. If Miss Lansing is threatening to kill you, I can take care of her. Now hand me the bag before someone gets hurt."

"Don't you understand? The only way to help Miss Lansing and her six-year-old little brother is to have me die. If not permanently, then for a short amount of time. Enough to give you and Riley a head start figuring out who has her brother and getting him back."

Refusing to release Riley, Mack faced the woman footing the bill for Declan's Defenders. Her heart was in the right place for most things, but defending a woman out to kill her was just plain crazy. "I can't let this woman go. If what you're saying is true, she came here to kill you." He frowned down at Riley. "How could you? This woman is responsible for saving your life."

Riley nodded. "Don't you think I know that?"

"Then why would you want to hurt her?" he asked.

Her shoulders sagged. "I had no other choice."

Mack shook his head. "There are always more choices."

"Not when it comes to her little brother," Charlie said.

"Since when do you have a little brother?" Mack's eyes narrowed. "You never mentioned a little brother."

Riley lifted her chin. "You don't know me well enough to ask."

"Does your roommate Grace know you have a little brother?" Mack asked.

Riley shook her head. "I don't advertise that part of my life. I thought I had him hidden away. I didn't think they would find out about him." She threw her hand in the air. "Hell, I thought they'd forgotten I even existed." She stared down at the arm clamped around her middle. "You can release me. I can't kill Mrs. Halverson. I just can't."

"Charlie," the older woman corrected. "Call me Charlie."

Riley gave her a weak smile. "See? How could I kill someone who is as kind and generous as Charlie?" She held out her hand. "Please, let me have the pill. I can't let it get into the wrong hands."

"Oh, but you've put it in exactly the right hands. I'm going to die tonight. And you're going to save your little brother," Charlie said.

"You are out of your mind." Mack released Riley and lunged for Charlie.

She backed toward the door, a frown pulling her brows together. "Listen, you two. We don't have much time."

Riley glanced at the watch on her wrist. "Time. Damn. I forgot. They gave me C-4 to set off as a diversion. I'm supposed to kill Mrs. Halverson and set off the explosive to create a diversion and allow me to escape. They're expecting the explosion."

"Good." Charlie smiled. "That will give us time to get my dead body out of the hotel and off to the morgue." Her smile faded. "As long as the explosion doesn't hurt anyone else."

"It shouldn't. I didn't use a lot of the explosive and I set it in a storeroom surrounded by other empty rooms. No one was there, and it was empty. No one should go back there."

"Wait a minute." Mack held up his hand. "I can't possibly be hearing this correctly. You can't set off explosives in a crowded hotel. It will start a stampede. Even if the explosion doesn't bring the walls down, the guests will rush for the doors and crush the people in front of them." Mack shook his head. "No. No. No. This is insane. Besides, I can't let you take that pill. If it's poison, what antidote is there? We don't even know what it is."

"I'm not going to take the pill, silly. I'm only going to pretend I did. You'll call for an ambulance. They'll wheel me out. Riley will escape and you'll go with her to help her find Toby, her little brother." Charlie drew in a deep breath and looked from Riley to Mack and back. "You see? All I have to do is lie dying in a hospital long enough for you two to find Toby and get him back."

Riley's eyes narrowed. "The instructions said the poison was fast-acting."

"So I didn't take all of it."

"They'll wait to give me Toby until they know for certain you're dead," Riley said.

"Money can buy just about anything," Charlie pointed out. "Even a fake death certificate."

"But they'll come looking for the body."

"So we'll give them one in the morgue."

"You seem to be forgetting something," Mack said.

"Am I?" Charlie frowned. "What am I forgetting?"

"You're not dead. You don't belong in a morgue until you are."

"Then you'll just have to find the boy while I'm lying on my deathbed in the hospital." Charlie crossed her arms over her chest.

"I don't like it," Mack said. "Why don't we go to the authorities and get them to find the boy?"

"The people who have him are Russian," Riley said. "They're not going to let the authorities find them or my brother. They'll move him out of the country. If they do, I'll never find him. As it is, I don't know where to begin looking. I don't know who my handler is." Riley's shoulders sagged. "Some Russian spy I am. I can't even take care of my own brother."

"Don't worry," Charlie said. "Follow my plan. Poison me, set off your explosion, let me play the dying matriarch and see what happens from there. What could it hurt? You get a few days' grace, and I get a rest in my husband's wing of the hospital. I can't see where this could possibly go wrong." She waved toward Riley. "Go ahead. Set off your explosion. You'll see."

Mack wasn't quite as sure as Charlie. And he'd rather have brought his men in to discuss what was going to happen, but Charlie had it in her head that her plan would work long enough for him and Riley to save her brother. She wouldn't be deterred.

"Where's the detonator?" Charlie asked.

Riley pointed to the ornamental hair clip lying on the counter near the sink. "But—"

"The longer you wait, the more suspicious your handler will become," Charlie pointed out. "Just do it and we'll take it from there."

"I don't know." Riley worried her handler would see through the plan.

"Have you worked with C-4 before now?" Mack asked.

Riley nodded. "But it's been years. Back when I lived with my parents. Before I went to college."

Mack gaped. "As a teen?"

Riley frowned. "I told you. I was trained to be a Russian sleeper spy. My parents prepared me for just about anything."

"I thought you were just an engineer..." He clapped a hand to his forehead. "Selling secret blueprints to your comrades?" He shook his head. "You were the one selling the top secret data to the Russians from Quest Aerospace?"

"No, of course not. I thought I was in the clear. That when my parents died, their handlers would forget about me." She snorted. "I was just another loyal American, trying to do good. Well, they didn't forget about me. They drew my number and tasked me to kill Mrs. Halverson."

"Charlie," the widow corrected.

"Charlie," Riley echoed. "They're using my brother as an insurance policy. They didn't give me a choice."

"Are you sure about the amount of plastics you used?" Mack asked.

"Pretty." She drew in a deep breath. "It should make a loud noise and shake the walls but not cause too much damage or a fire."

"For the record…" He caught Charlie's glance. "I don't like any of this."

"So noted." Charlie gave him a mock salute. "But you're going to go along with it?"

Mack nodded and touched his hand to his headset. "Guys, be ready to lead the guests in an orderly exodus from the hotel," he said.

"Did you say what I think you said?" Gus questioned.

"What are you talking about?" Mustang asked.

"Can't say," Mack said. "Just be ready." Then he nodded to Charlie. "Assume the position."

Charlie grinned and sank to the floor in her expensive gown.

"You can't smile if you're dying," Mack warned her.

The smile disappeared from her face and she closed her eyes. "Ready."

"I'm calling the ambulance," Mack said, and dialed 911. He turned to Riley, not sure he should trust her, but knowing it was what Charlie wanted and possibly the only way to get the woman out of the hotel safely if others were gunning for her. "As soon as they say the fire department is on its way, let 'er rip."

Mack reported a woman down to the dispatcher. Once he was assured the ambulance was on its way, he nodded toward Riley.

She lifted the ornamental hair clip and activated the switch on the back.

A thundering *bang* rippled through the heavy doors of the restroom.

Muffled screams sounded.

"The guests are moving toward the doors on the west side," Gus reported.

"And on the north and east," Mustang confirmed. "So far, they're moving swiftly without panic. The security staff are facilitating their efforts. Where are you and Charlie?"

"In the ladies' restroom on the southern end of

the ballroom," Mack said. "If the exodus is moving well, Mustang, I need you here to take over for me. When the ambulance arrives, Gus, lead them into the restroom to collect Charlie."

"What happened? Is she all right?" Mustang asked.

"No." Mack stared across the room to where Charlie lay on the floor with her eyes open. "She's been poisoned. I have to leave, but I need you and Gus to stick with her like glue and keep her safe. Someone wants her dead. If she lives through the poison, they might not let her live to leave the hospital."

Chapter Three

"Riley, you need to leave the restroom before anyone arrives," Charlie said.

Mack's eyes narrowed. "I don't know that I trust her to leave without me. And I can't leave until Mustang gets here to protect you."

"I'll wait for you inside the doorway near the end of this hallway," Riley said.

"How do I know you won't take off?" Mack said.

"I have to find my brother, and I need help doing it. But I don't want you to leave Charlie alone, either. She's done so much for me already. I couldn't live with myself if someone finished what I was supposed to start."

Mack's lips thinned. "I don't trust you. But more than that, I won't leave Charlie." He jerked his head to the side. "Go. I'll catch up with you."

He didn't have to say it, but he meant he'd catch

up to her whether she waited for him at the end of the hallway or not. His tone said he'd hunt her down if he had to.

Riley shivered at the killer glare Mack gave her.

Though she knew how to stop a two-hundred-fifty-pound man dead in his tracks and could cripple her foe in one easy sweep of her leg, her knees turned to jelly at just one look from the tall, dark-haired marine. He frightened her more than her mysterious Russian handler. And it wasn't so much Mack's demeanor and strength. It was the way he'd made her feel when he wrapped his arm around her waist. He made her feel feminine and vulnerable. She couldn't afford to feel vulnerable. Not when the stakes were so high.

If she were the only one at risk, she wouldn't be as concerned. But Toby depended on her to find and rescue him. And Charlie...the woman who'd helped her so selflessly on more than one occasion. She owed the woman more than her life. She owed her loyalty and respect. Whoever wanted her dead wouldn't stop until the wealthy widow was six feet in the ground.

Why?

Mack moved to the door and peered out. "The hallway is empty. If you go now, you won't be seen."

Riley didn't have time to contemplate all the questions roiling around in her head. She had to get out of the restroom before Mack's buddies descended on him to discover why he'd given them such cryptic instructions in anticipation of an explosion. They had to be filled with questions he wouldn't have time to answer.

Riley eased up to the door and stood beside the big marine.

He smelled of aftershave and seemed larger than life in his black tuxedo with the crisp white shirt peeking out from between the jacket's lapels. Beneath the fancy clothes, the man was handsome in a rugged way that made her heart flutter.

He jerked open the door. "Go."

Riley startled and rushed through. The hem of her dress caught on the door and ripped the side seam farther up her leg. She grabbed the fabric and gave it a quick tug, freeing it from the corner of the door. Then she lifted the folds in her hands and ran as fast as she could in three-inch heels. Racing down the hallway, she ducked into the room she'd found during her reconnaissance a day earlier.

The room had two doors. One leading out into the hallway, the other leading toward the kitchen and the service elevators. If she'd done what she was supposed to do and actually killed Charlotte Halverson, she'd be sprinting to get out of the hotel, out of DC and back to her Virginia apartment, where she'd pretend she'd never left.

Her roommate had indicated she'd be with Declan

O'Neill, Mack's team leader, for a mini vacation to the Outer Banks of North Carolina. Lucky her, she'd fallen in love with the man who'd helped her find and protect Riley when her brief stint assisting the FBI nearly gotten her killed. She still couldn't believe that her Russian handler had called her to action on an assassination, not on the data she'd developed dealing with a revolutionary aircraft design. She'd have thought they'd demand the design in exchange for her brother.

Perhaps the assassination was their way of compromising her so much she'd be forced to hand over the blueprints for the special project she'd been working on at Quest Aerospace Alliance. She wouldn't have a choice if they threatened to expose her to the authorities.

Was that it? Was her handler someone she knew at Quest? Was that where her search should begin?

She waited for two, maybe three, minutes for Mack to appear. The time stretched, feeling like half an hour instead of the few short minutes. If she didn't leave soon, and her handler was watching for her exit, he might begin to wonder about her success.

Riley glanced at the pretty watch on her wrist and realized it had only been two minutes since she'd left the ladies' room. She'd give Mack one more minute before she had to leave. Soon, the entire building would be locked down, with police and firefighters swarming over the structure. They wouldn't have the opportunity to leave at that point.

She eased the door open and nearly screamed at the face appearing in front of her.

"Come on, we have to get out of here," Mack said. "The police are coming through the lobby now." He took her hand and tried to lead her back the way she'd come.

"No. This way." She dug her heels into the carpet and dragged him into the little room and across to the door on the other side.

"Do you know where you're going?" he asked.

"Yes. Through the kitchen and out to the loading docks."

Mack followed, still holding her hand as he let her take the lead. "I didn't think you'd wait."

"I almost didn't," she whispered. "Now, shh." She raised her free hand to press a finger to her lips. "There's a camera located at the rear entrance. I came in this way as a blonde. I'd rather not have the camera catch us leaving."

"Can I reach it?" Mack asked.

Riley gave him a measured glance. "Maybe."

He pulled a handkerchief from his inside pocket. "With this?"

She tilted her head and shook it. "There's a breeze. It'll blow away if you try to throw it over the camera lens."

Mack glanced around the loading dock and took off. "I'll be right back." He made a beeline for a shop sink in the corner, wet the handkerchief and returned. "Let's do this. We don't have much time."

Riley stepped aside. "Go."

Mack peered up at the camera located on the wall over the back door to the loading dock. It pointed at the door and the loading bays where trucks backed in to discharge the supplies needed to keep a hotel as big as the Marriott in business.

With a flick of his wrist, Mack slung the wet hanky up over the camera. It caught, covering the lens.

Riley released the breath she hadn't realized she'd been holding. Without another word, she led the way from the hotel out onto the pavement and pushed through the bushes into the back lot of an office building.

"Where to from here?" Mack asked.

"I parked my car two blocks over."

"You really thought this through, didn't you?" His tone held an edge to it.

"I had to. My brother's life depends on it." She didn't wait for him to follow but took off, walking fast. Part of her wanted to leave him behind. His tone held judgment. She deserved his scorn but didn't want to deal with it. "We don't have much time. My handler will likely discover Mrs. Halverson isn't dead and demand I finish the job or Toby will pay the price. The sooner we find my brother, the sooner we can get him out of danger."

"And once you have your brother, your handler will allow you to walk free?"

Riley snorted. "No way. I'll have to take Toby and go into hiding somewhere far from here."

"Seems to me we need to put a stop to your handler as well as find your brother."

"Agreed, but most importantly, I need to find my brother." She stepped through another bush, her dress catching on the branches.

Mack helped her untangle the fabric and pushed through behind her. They came to the back of a building that appeared to be abandoned. A small charcoal-gray four-door sedan was tucked between a stack of pallets and a trash bin.

Riley reached beneath the second pallet in the stack, extracted a key fob and hurried toward the vehicle.

When she pulled the handle on the sedan, the doors unlocked.

Mack climbed into the passenger seat as Riley started the engine. He was putting his safety belt on when she pulled out from behind the building and raced out onto the street.

"Get a speeding ticket and you draw attention to yourself," Mack warned.

Riley eased up on the accelerator. "I don't know

where to start. I have no idea who my handler is and how I can find him," she admitted.

"Start from when you received the message with the instructions."

She drove toward her apartment, not knowing where else to go. At least there she could change into more appropriate clothing for finding another Russian spy.

Hysterical laughter bubbled up her throat and threatened to escape. What did one wear when searching for a spy?

Mack whipped his head around. "You just ran a red light. Do you want me to drive?"

Riley pulled to the side of the street, got out and rounded the car to Mack's side.

He stepped out and held the door for her.

As she sank into the passenger seat, silent tears spilled down her cheeks.

Mack didn't say a word, just got in and drove. He knew where she lived from when Grace had invited the team to the apartment to celebrate their little victory.

Victory, hell. Perhaps Riley's little venture with the FBI had brought her back to the attention of her parents' handler. If she hadn't gotten so entrenched in her American life and started thinking she'd been forgotten, she might not be in her current situation, and Toby would be safe in the country cabin with his nanny.

Mack pulled into the parking lot of Riley and Grace's apartment building and turned off the engine. For a long moment, he sat beside her, letting her gather herself.

A hand reached out and touched her arm. "We should go inside."

Riley nodded. "I'm not usually so weepy," she said, and sniffed. "Only when it comes to my family. I love my brother. He's such a good little boy." She looked across the console at Mack. "He doesn't know who we are or what the Russians will want from me. He's just a little boy who plays with toys."

Mack nodded and held her gaze for another moment. Then he reached out and brushed his thumb across her cheek, wiping away the tears. "We'll find him."

"How?" she asked, her voice catching on a sob.

"There has to be a trail. We'll follow it. But we can't do it dressed like this. Go. Change and then we'll hit my apartment long enough for me to get out of this monkey suit. Then we'll get to work sifting through the clues." He unfolded his long frame from the driver's seat and rounded the hood to open the door for her.

Riley had the door open. When she stepped out,

her heel caught on her dress, and she pitched forward into Mack's chest.

His arms came up around her and held her steady until she could work her heel free of the hem. She straightened, still in Mack's embrace, and looked up into his incredibly blue eyes. A streetlight shone down, making his dark hair glow a silvery blue. "Thanks."

"My pleasure," he replied. Still, he didn't release her. "How does one become a sleeper spy for the Russians?"

She gave a short, sharp burst of laughter. "You're born into it, and your parents raise you with their beliefs."

"But you attended American schools and speak perfect American English."

"I'm American, through and through. I didn't sign on to be a Russian spy. I thought when my parents died, I was off the hook. Their handler wouldn't remember the little girl they gave birth to shortly after their arrival in the US." Riley rested her hand on his chest and stared at the crisp white shirt beneath her fingertips. "I never wanted to be a Russian spy."

"But you learned about C-4 explosives," Mack prompted.

Riley sighed. "And weaponry, guns, hand-to-hand combat and how to pick locks. Every skill a spy would need to survive."

His lips twitched. "You're scaring me."

"My father was with the KGB before he brought my mother to the States. He knew all the tricks."

"But your little brother is only six years old? That's a big age gap between you and him."

"He was a late surprise to my parents in their forties. I'd just begun working for Quest when my mother told me she was pregnant."

"Where are your parents now?"

"They died in an automobile accident when Toby was only one year old."

"Which left you to raise him," Mack concluded.

"Only, I didn't want the Russians to know about him. Any more than they did. I moved him to a cabin in the country, and hired a nanny to live with him full time. I visited him as often as I could. I'd just started working on the Special Projects team at Quest. If I left, I was afraid anyone watching me would follow me to Toby." She snorted. "Apparently I wasn't careful enough. They found him anyway."

Riley led the way to her town house apartment. The damaged doorframe and broken window had been replaced from when the apartment was invaded by an intruder searching for her research memory card two weeks prior. She held the door for Mack, but he stopped inside the threshold, with the door open.

"Are you going to stand there, or come in?" she asked.

He leaned close and whispered in her ear, "If someone is watching you, you need to convince them I'm not a threat."

She frowned up at him. "And how do you intend to do that?" she asked, matching his low tones.

He nuzzled her neck and breathed into her ear, "They need to think I'm supposed to be with you."

She tipped her head back and closed her eyes, all the while keeping her voice down. If she was being watched, they might also be employing some kind of listening device. "We don't want them to think you're a bodyguard or coconspirator, do we?" She shook her head. "They know I don't have any other siblings, and I've never known any cousins."

"What about a boyfriend?" Mack suggested, running his hand up beneath her hair. "Are you known to have a boyfriend or lover?"

Butterflies erupted in Riley's belly at the touch of his hand on the back of her neck. "No. I haven't had time to cultivate a romance. I've been too busy living two lives to add another to the mix."

He leaned back and smiled down into her eyes. "Then let's set the stage for anyone watching."

"What do you mean?" She stiffened, her insides trembling, her body warming with excitement.

"Meet your new boyfriend."

MACK TOOK HER hand in his and gave it a gentle tug. If, like he suspected, her handler had eyes and ears posted wherever Riley lived or worked, they had to convince the watchers they were an item. Otherwise, why would he be at her apartment that late at night?

She came to him, rested her hands on his jacket and raised her face to his. "Like this?"

"Uh-huh," he whispered. "Only closer." He slipped an arm around her waist and pulled her ever nearer until he couldn't tell where her body ended and his began. Her breasts pressed against the lapels of his jacket, and her hands fluttered against his chest. The back of her gown dipped low, and his hands met warm, bare skin.

With one hand on her back, steadying her, he used the other to tip her chin. Then he lowered his mouth to just above hers. "We need to make it convincing."

"Okay," Riley said, her voice barely a breath. Then her tongue swept across her lips, making them shine in the light over the door.

What had started as a show for anyone watching had taken on a life of its own. Mack couldn't look away from her shining lips any more than he could drop his hold. He was destined to kiss this woman who could be a national spy. Hell, she'd come to the charity event to kill the woman he worked for. Why would he be drawn to an assassin?

But he was, and he had to kiss her.

Cupping her cheek, he bent to brush his lips lightly across hers. They were soft. Like silk.

She gasped, and her mouth opened, giving him all the invitation he needed.

He swept his tongue past her teeth to claim hers in a long, sensual caress that made his insides ignite and his groin tighten.

Her fingers curled into his shirt, bringing him closer, deepening the kiss. Her hips pressed against his, his erection nudging against the soft folds of the dress covering her belly.

Mack groaned and lowered his other arm, crushing her to him. When he was forced to breathe again, he reluctantly loosened his hold enough to allow air in their lungs.

He inhaled deeply and pressed his forehead to hers. "That should do the trick," he said, wondering at the tremor in his voice.

She closed her eyes and pressed her lips together. Then she straightened and stepped back.

Mack dropped his arms from around her waist, planted one in the center of her back and entered the apartment, kicking the door closed behind them. He would never admit to Riley that the kiss had shaken him as much as it had. He wasn't with her to start an affair. He'd been tasked by his employer to help Riley find her brother. The sooner they did, the sooner he'd be on to his next assignment.

Chapter Four

Mack waited in the living room of Riley's apartment while she changed out of the dress she'd worn to the gala.

She left the door to her bedroom cracked open a little—to continue their conversation or to keep an eye on him, Mack wasn't sure.

He searched the apartment for any signs of listening devices or cameras. Just when he thought he was chasing shadows, he found something in one of the lamps sitting on an end table. He was reaching for it when Riley came out of the bedroom pulling a light sweater down her torso. "You know, I think I know where we should start."

Mack spun toward her, grabbed her arms and pulled her into his embrace. "I know exactly where we should start." Then he sealed her mouth with his lips.

"What—" Riley tried to say as his lips moved over hers.

She stood stiff in his arms until he softened the kiss and swept his hands down her back.

After a long, incredibly delicious moment, he lifted his head, pressed a finger to her lips and led her over to the lamp. He pointed to the small electronics device positioned on one of the wires holding the shade in place. Then he pointed to his ear. "I think we should start with a kiss," he said softly, but loudly enough for whoever might be listening in on their conversation.

Riley's eyes widened and then narrowed. She tilted her head toward the bedroom. "Maybe we should take this into the bedroom," she said in a sultry tone.

Riley took Mack's hand and led him into the bedroom, where they performed a thorough search of every nook and cranny.

Another electronic device turned up in the lamp on her nightstand and one more on the light fixture in the bathroom.

Her lips thinning with each step, Riley marched to the closet, grabbed a suitcase and stuffed it with clothing.

Mack couldn't blame her. Her space had been broken into before, but this was even worse. Someone had been spying on her with every word spoken. He checked behind the paintings on the walls and on the bookshelves just in case he found a video camera. He even stood on a chair and looked in the overhead light fixtures. Thankfully, there weren't any camcorders lurking. But he might have missed one.

When Riley was dressed in jeans and tennis shoes and had a bag packed with clothes and toiletries, she led the way to the door.

Mack opened it for her and they exited the town house.

"You want to drive?" she asked.

Since he still had the keys, he nodded. As soon as they were out of the parking lot, he turned toward his apartment. "I just want to change into something a little less confining than this." He waved a hand toward his tuxedo. "I have to admit, this is my first time in a tux."

"Really?" She tilted her head and studied him. "You wear it well."

"Thanks. But don't get used to it. I'm a jeans and T-shirt kind of guy."

"My preference," she said.

"In guys, or clothes?" he asked.

Riley smiled. "Both."

They accomplished the trip to his apartment in relative silence. After discovering three listening devices in her apartment, Mack didn't trust her car, either. When he arrived in his parking lot, he held the door for Riley and helped her out of her sedan, handing her the keys.

"You aren't driving from here?" she asked.

"Not in yours." He cupped her elbow and led her toward his apartment. Once they were out of listening range of her vehicle, he relaxed a little. "I think we'll take my vehicle from here."

"You think they had bugs in my car as well?" She grimaced. "Did we say anything that would lead them to think we weren't on the up-and-up?"

"I don't remember. But we'd do well to keep our conversations down to a whisper when we discuss the plan."

"We have a plan?" She looked up at him, her eyebrow cocked.

"We will," he said. "As soon as I get out of this suit."

"Right."

She followed him into his apartment, her gaze sweeping across the furniture and bare walls. "Are you one of those minimalists?"

He smiled. "No. I just moved in. Since I'm new to the area, I'm not even sure this is where I want to stay."

"It's an okay neighborhood, from what I could see in the dark."

"I prefer the countryside to city life. But my work with Charlie brings me to the city."

"How long have you worked for Charlie?"

He twisted his lips into a wry smile. "Two whole weeks."

"And before that? Were you one of Declan's teammates in the military?"

He nodded.

"What's the deal with you guys? Grace said you were basically kicked out."

Mack shut the door and twisted the dead bolt. "She's right. Dishonorable discharges."

"Seriously? Don't you have to be like the worst of the worst to get one of those?"

He shrugged. "I guess we are."

"What did you do to warrant dishonorable discharge?"

"We didn't follow through on our orders. The man we were supposed to kill got away and killed some important people because of it."

"Still…seems pretty drastic to get kicked out."

"We made a decision we could live with." If he had to make the same decision again, he'd do so.

"Did you think it would get you kicked out?"

Again, he shrugged. "No. But politics were involved."

"So you took the fall for someone higher up?"

"Maybe. Or maybe refusing a direct order was enough." Mack agreed, but what was done was done. Someone needed scapegoats. Their team took the fall. They were out of the Marine Corps, and life went on. "If we hadn't been kicked out, I wouldn't be here with you now. We can leave it at that."

"Okay." She walked to the window overlooking a park.

Mack left her in the living room and went to his bedroom to change. His gaze took in the sparse furnishings from Riley's perspective. He hadn't made the apartment his home. In fact, since joining the military, he hadn't made any living arrangements like home. He didn't stay in one place very long. The Marine Corps had a way of moving you often. Why put down roots and hang pictures on the wall when you'd just have to pull the nails out and move to another station or be deployed for half a year or more?

"You know, it might be a little late to ask, but are you married or anything?" Riley asked from the other side of the wall.

"I wouldn't have kissed you like I did if I was," Mack said. He pulled the jacket off and laid it across the end of the bed. Then the shoulder holster he'd worn beneath with the P226 handgun. "Call me old-fashioned, but if I were married, I wouldn't kiss another woman."

"Even if it was part of an undercover operation?" Riley asked.

"Even then." Maybe he wasn't cut out for undercover operations. If he ever married, he'd have to stick to bodyguard duties and leave the undercover shtick to the other members of the team.

"I'm impressed," Riley said. "My father would

have insisted I do whatever it took to keep my cover. Even if it meant sleeping with the enemy."

"And have you?"

"This was my first assignment. And I didn't want it in the first place. If not for Toby, I wouldn't be in this situation. I'd have refused."

"Do the Russians allow you to refuse?"

She didn't answer for a moment. And then her voice came back softly. "I don't know. According to my father, we had no other choice. I'm beginning to believe him. I just wonder what they held over him. He seemed happy in his American life. Like he'd fully embraced the life, liberty and justice of the American dream. He had a good-paying job with a local factory, using his skills as an engineer to make parts for tractors and combines. If you'd met him, you'd never have known he was KGB. He had no accent that gave him away."

Mack shucked his white dress shirt, changed out of the tuxedo trousers into a pair of dark jeans, and stepped into the bedroom doorframe. "What about your mother?"

Riley looked up, her eyes widening. She swallowed hard and swept her tongue across her lips before replying, "Also Russian, but raised by an American au pair." As if tearing her gaze away from his bare chest, she turned back to the window. "My mother must have taught my father how to speak American English."

"And yet she let him train you to be a sleeper

spy?" Mack slipped a black T-shirt over his head and tugged it over his shoulders and torso.

"Maybe she thought since we were in the States, they wouldn't be called on to complete any missions. That was my hope, too. Especially after my folks died. I thought they'd forget I existed and leave me alone." She looked back over her shoulder with a weak smile. "I guess I was wrong." Her eyes were glassy with unshed tears. "And Toby is paying the price for my mistake."

Mack padded across the carpet, wrapped her in his arms. If she didn't want him to hold her, she could have taken him down like the professionally trained spy she was. Instead, she leaned her face against his chest and let the tears slip down her cheeks.

"My father would be so very disappointed in me right now," she said, and sniffed.

Mack brushed his lips across the top of her head, reveling in how soft and silky her black hair was. And it smelled of wildflowers. He inhaled deeply. "We'll find him," he promised. He wasn't sure how they'd do that, but he'd do his best to make good on that vow. He wanted to help this woman. She was a stranger to him, but he felt a connection that had nothing to do with the job.

RILEY'S HEAD SPUN in a thousand directions as she thought hard about where to start looking for Toby.

The enormity of the effort threatened to over-whelm her. The hard muscles beneath Riley's palms strangely reassured her, like a rock in a fast-moving stream. He grounded her. This man had promised to find her little brother. They were smart people. To-gether they would figure it out.

For a long moment, she let herself lean on him, al-lowed her tears to flow while absorbing his strength.

He tilted her head up and stared down into her eyes. "We have to think through your life. There has to be someone in it who has been monitoring your every move. Possibly someone close to you."

She drew in a deep breath and nodded. "I thought it was my supervisor at Quest. But he's dead, killed by the people who wanted the data from my spe-cial project."

"Does anyone else at Quest hang around you a lot? Do you have any friends who seem really inter-ested in you and your life?"

Riley didn't move from Mack's arms. Instead, she stared at her hands on his black T-shirt and thought through all the people she came into contact with on a daily basis. None stuck out more than the others.

"What about your roommate?"

"Grace?" Riley frowned. "No way. I met her my first year at Georgetown University."

Mack's brows rose. "And you were together for the entire four years?"

Riley's frown deepened. "Yes, but she's with Declan now. And she got Mrs. Halverson involved in finding me. She's too nice. She couldn't be a Russian spy." She shook her head. "No, it wasn't Grace. My gut tells me no."

"And you trust your gut." Mack nodded. "My gut has saved me on more than one occasion."

"I need to talk with Margaret Weems, Toby's nanny. She might have seen something. And we have a security system at the house. I want to review the footage. I usually have access from my cell phone, but the connection has been interrupted. I have to find out why."

"You're not due back at work until Monday."

"If Mrs. H. hasn't died by then, it might be too late for Toby."

"Then we have to hurry through the leads we have." Mack set her at arm's length. "Are you okay?"

She snorted softly. "Do I have a choice? I have to be okay in order to find Toby. I'm all he has."

"Now he has me, too." With his thumb, he brushed away a tear. "Let's do this. Where is this cabin? Sounds like we need to make a trip there."

Riley checked her watch. "It's two hours outside the city in the Virginia countryside. With the amount of construction on the roads between here and there, by the time we get there, it'll be morning. Margaret will be beside herself. I haven't contacted her since the abduction."

"Then we start there. Just you showing up will help her."

"I doubt it. She blames herself for his disappearance. She thinks she should have heard the intruder."

"Let's get out there. We can question her."

"It's a small town. If a stranger came through, someone might have seen him."

"And someone might have security cameras on their shops. We could ask to see them."

Riley nodded. "It's like sifting through a haystack looking for one specific strand of straw."

"All it takes is that one," Mack said. "We just have to find it."

Mack disappeared into his bedroom and reappeared a few minutes later wearing boots and a black leather jacket. The bulge beneath it indicated he was wearing more than a shirt under the leather.

Once again, his presence gave Riley hope.

He held out his hand.

Riley placed hers in his. "Why are you doing this?"

"For one, it's my job."

"Is that the only reason?"

He shook his head. "Let's just say I had a little brother once. I would have done anything to save him."

Riley walked with Mack to a big black pickup.

He helped her up into the passenger seat and then rounded the hood to the driver's side.

She gave him the address to the cabin. He punched it into his GPS and soon they were on a highway leading out of Alexandria into the countryside. As she settled back in her seat, she thought about what he'd said about his little brother. "You said *had*. You had a little brother." She glanced across the console at the man behind the wheel. "What happened to your little brother?"

His lips thinned into a straight line. "He didn't make it past six years old."

Riley drew in a sharp breath, her chest squeezing tightly. "What happened to him?"

For a long moment, Mack didn't answer. His face grew even darker in the light from the dash. "We were waiting at our rural bus stop when he stepped out in front of a logging truck."

"Oh my God." Riley cover her mouth with her hand. Her stomach roiled at the image conjured by his words. "And you saw it happen?"

"I was standing next to him one minute," Mack said. "The next minute he was gone."

"And you thought it was your fault," Riley said. She could see the truth in the way his hands gripped the steering wheel so tightly his knuckles turned white. He blamed himself for his brother's death.

"I should have held his hand. But I was older and didn't think it was cool."

"You couldn't know he'd dart out into the street."

"It doesn't matter now," Mack said. "Nothing I can do now will bring Aiden back. But I will find Toby for you. We will get him back. Alive."

Riley sat back, her heart hurting for Mack's little brother and the young man Mack had been when he lost him. The miles passed.

Riley must have fallen asleep. The smooth road turned bumpy, shaking her awake. She opened her eyes to the gray light of dawn pushing the darkness out of the sky. In front of her was the little cabin she'd rented when she moved Toby out to the country with his nanny, Margaret. The idea was to keep him hidden from her potential handlers. Now she wondered if she'd have been better off keeping him in the city, close to her. At least then she would have had a chance to fight off his kidnapper.

As they pulled up to the house, Toby's nanny, an older woman with graying hair, appeared in the door. She stared out at them, her eyes narrowed.

Riley climbed down from the truck. "Oh, Margaret."

The woman's eyes widened, and she cried out. "Riley!" She ran out on the porch and down the steps.

Riley met her halfway to the house and was wrapped in the older woman's huge hug.

"Oh, Riley," she sobbed. "I'm so sorry. I don't

know how it happened. I've been beside myself since Toby disappeared. Please tell me you know what's going on. Tell me he's all right." She backed away far enough to look Riley in the face. Her lips trembled, and tears spilled from her eyes. "You haven't heard from him, have you? Oh, sweet heaven. My little guy is gone."

"Margaret." Riley cupped the nanny's cheek. "We'll find him. But we came to see if there's any images on the security system and to ask questions. We hope to find some clues."

"Why don't you contact the police? I've lifted the phone a hundred times and put it down." She wrung her hands. "We should call them. They'll know what to do."

Riley bracketed the woman's face between her hands. "Margaret, we can't call the police. The kidnapper will hurt Toby if we do."

"What does he want?" she said, her tone like a wail. "It's not like you're rich."

"He wants me to do something I don't want to do."

"Do it," Margaret urged. "Get Toby back."

"I can't talk about it. You have to trust me. I'm doing everything in my power to find Toby."

Margaret pulled a tissue out of her pocket and pressed it to her nose. "I just don't understand how this could happen."

"I'm going to check the cameras and the recordings. While I do that, talk to my friend Mack. He's here to help. Answer his questions, if you can. Anything you might have seen could help us find Toby. No matter how insignificant it might seem."

"Okay." Margaret looked from Riley to Mack. "Ask away. I hope I know something that will help."

Riley nodded to Mack. "I'll be inside looking through the footage."

"We'll join you," Mack said. "We can look and ask questions at the same time."

Mack followed the women into the cabin. He paused for a moment on the threshold and stared out at the woods surrounding the little house. Then he turned and joined the women around a computer monitor at a small desk in the corner of the main bedroom.

Riley wiggled the mouse and waited for the screen to come alive. When it didn't, she turned the screen on, then off. Nothing.

Then she turned the computer off, then on. Nothing happened; the motor didn't kick on and the fans that usually hummed inside were silent. The computer was dead.

"How long has the computer been dead?" Riley asked.

"I was online the morning before Toby disappeared. I haven't touched it since. I searched the entire house and the yard. I even went into the woods along the paths we usually walk. I thought he might have wandered away."

"He didn't wander away, Margaret. He's definitely been taken. The man who took him put him on the phone to prove it."

Tears welled in the nanny's eyes. "Poor baby. He must be so scared."

Riley's heart contracted at the trauma her little brother was experiencing. She hardened herself to the inevitable. She couldn't take that away from him, but she could bring him back. "Tell me about the day before Toby disappeared. I need to know where you went, who you talked to, anyone different you might have run into in town."

"It was a regular day. Toby had school in the morning. I took him, dropped him off and went to the store to pick up a few groceries."

"Did you see anyone in town that you hadn't seen before?" Mack asked.

Margaret frowned, her eyes narrowing as she thought back. "I can't remember seeing anyone different. It's such a small town, you'd think I'd notice. If anyone would know, it would be Janice at the convenience store. She's where everyone goes for the local gossip, since the store is at the center of town and you have to pass it to get anywhere in or out of Havenwood. You should ask Janice."

"We will," Riley said. "And I'll take this computer with me in case I can find someone who can fix it."

Margaret touched Riley's arm. "Please, find Toby. I'm completely lost without that child. He's such a ray of sunshine. I can't imagine anyone wanting to hurt him."

"We will," Riley said. She prayed she was right. She'd hoped the trip to the cabin would yield some small clue. But so far, nothing, and their time was running out.

Chapter Five

Mack reached across the console and grasped Riley's hand as they left the cabin and drove into the little town of Havenwood. "We'll find him," he reassured her, though he wasn't feeling as confident as he had when he drove up to the cabin.

"How can we find him when we have nothing to go on?"

"We'll talk with this Janice woman. She has to have seen something."

"And if she hasn't?" Riley stared through the windshield, her hand squeezing his tightly.

"Then we ask someone else." He entered the town, passed a diner that had cars parked outside. His stomach growled, reminding him that they hadn't eaten breakfast. In fact, he hadn't had anything to eat since lunch the day before. He would bet Riley hadn't had anything since she'd gotten the message from the kidnapper. After they talked with Janice, they'd stop in at the diner and have a bite. Waitresses always seemed to have the scoop of what was going on in town.

Mack pulled up to the gas pump at the only convenience store in Havenwood. Riley went inside while he filled the truck's tank.

Once he was finished, he entered to find Riley in deep conversation with the woman behind the counter.

"Yes, we do get people passing through occasionally," the woman said.

Riley turned to smile at Mack. "Janice, this is Mack, my…boyfriend." She turned back to Janice. "Janice was just telling me how nice it is to live in such a small town. She knows everyone, and everyone knows her."

"I've seen Riley here just about every weekend, but she never said anything about you." Janice eyed Mack, her gaze sweeping him from head to toe. "I wouldn't forget a good-looking guy like you." She held out her hand, her cheeks growing pinker. "Nope, I wouldn't forget you."

Mack took her hand and gave her one of the smiles he reserved for pretty girls at the bar. "Nice to meet you, Janice." He gripped her hand with a firm handshake.

"Ooh, and his hands are so strong." Janice grinned at Riley. "You're one lucky girl to have him as your guy."

Riley touched Mack's arm. "I know." She faced Janice. "I bet from your location you see all the people who pass through Havenwood."

The store owner nodded. "I do. I can tell you every vehicle that goes through this town." She tapped a finger to her temple. "I have a photographic memory. And I like to play games with the license plates. It helps me to remember them. Like just three days ago, an out-of-towner came through with Maryland license plates that spelled WMD 495."

Mack tensed. "You remember that?"

She nodded. "What does WMD stand for to you?"

"Weapons of mass destruction," Mack answered.

Janice frowned. "I guess it could be that, too, but I thought *what Mama does.* And 495 is my niece's birthday. April 9, 2005. So, you see, the game helps me remember plates. You never know when you might need to identify them for the police. Knock on wood." She knocked on her skull.

Riley leaned on the counter, giving Janice all her attention. "I bet you can remember every type of car with the license plates that have passed through Havenwood in the past three days."

"Sure can." Janice crossed her arms over her chest. "Go ahead, try me."

"Three days ago, WMD 495 came through. What kind of vehicle was it?" Riley challenged.

"Silver Toyota Prius. I remember because I thought it was a silly car. My mother wouldn't have driven it. It wasn't big enough. She likes driving big boats of cars."

"Do you remember the driver in the vehicle?"

Janice frowned. "If he hadn't gotten out and come in, I couldn't have told you. The windows were heavily tinted." She closed her eyes. "And there was a bumper sticker on the back. I think it was for one of the car rental companies."

"Any others come through?" Mack asked. "Your memory amazes me."

"A bright red Mustang convertible with an older couple in it." Janice tipped her head. "Virginia license plate KNT 552. I think of KNT as *knit* and 552 as five-feet-two-inch girl like me. See how easy it is to play?" She gave them a triumphant smile.

"Was that all that came through that day? What about the day before?"

She tapped a finger to her temple and stared into the corner of the store. "We had a delivery truck from Maryland stop on its way to the next town, and one of those smart cars that was so tiny it could have been a child's toy. I remember it because it had the same colors as my favorite hockey team. Green and white."

"So, the driver of the WMD vehicle got out of his car?"

"Actually, he did. He came into the store. He had wavy dark hair and heavy eyebrows." Janice clapped her hands. "I can prove it. I recently had a security system installed. Got a deal from Henry last month. Got the whole thing put in for under five hundred. Wanna see? It's the coolest."

Riley gave a casual shrug. "Sure."

Inside, Mack would bet, she was shaking with excitement. This could be a clue they'd been looking for.

Janice turned a monitor around so that they could look at the images as she worked the keyboard. "It's the easiest thing to do. All I have to do is slide the bar back to the date and time I want and voilà!" She pointed to the date and time on the bottom corner of the screen. "See? Three days ago, around four in the evening. There's the car, just like I said, with the license plate WMD 495." Janice pointed to one of the images. "And there he is entering the store." She enlarged the image of the man. "I remember thinking he could use a haircut."

"Do you mind if I take a picture of the screen? I'm thinking of installing a security system and I like this one," Riley said.

"Go ahead." Janice waved toward the monitor.

Riley held up her cell phone and snapped a picture of the man in the image and the license plate of the vehicle in the other image.

"Janice, you have a good memory," Mack said. "I'm impressed."

The store owner blushed and shrugged. "That was all I had before this fancy-schmancy security system. That and the height gauge on the side of the doors." She nodded toward what appeared to be a measuring tool on either side of the door, indicating the height of those who entered and left. "You can't be too careful these days."

"No kidding."

"By the way, how's Toby?" Janice asked. "He usually comes in with you."

Riley didn't miss a beat with her answer. "He's visiting a relative."

"He's such a good little boy when he comes into the store with Margaret. Such good manners. They were here the same day as that man I described." She moved the slide button to a few minutes later. Toby and Margaret entered the store. Toby ran to the candy aisle ahead of Margaret.

"He likes chocolate. Margaret gets him a little bite of something every time they come in."

Riley's smile slipped, and her jaw tightened as she watched Toby.

Mack studied the little store and noted that the man with the dark hair from the car with the WMD license plate stood at the end of the same row as Toby. He stared at a display of snacks, but he didn't take anything.

Mack's hands clenched into fists. The jerk was watching the kid.

Margaret came up behind Toby, selected a candy bar from the rack and led Toby by the hand to Janice, the cashier.

"My, my hair was a mess that day," Janice said. "I'm surprised I didn't scare anyone." She patted her hair and turned the monitor back to face her behind the counter. "Anyway, you didn't come in to learn all about me and my monitoring system. What can I help you with?"

"Nothing really. I just never stop and chat when I come through," Riley said. "However, I would like one of your iced drinks." She removed her wallet from her purse. "What do I owe you?"

Janice filled a cup with ice and the soda of Riley's choice and rang up her purchase. "I'm glad you stopped by. We don't get too many visitors stopping for longer than to fill up their gas tank."

"Did the man with the WMD license plate come back through again?"

"I thought he was just passing through, but he must have stayed nearby. I was looking through my recordings the next day, playing with the date-time feature, and noticed he came through again late that night." Janice shrugged. "Must have been visiting one of our residents to be leaving that late. Or early... depending on how you look at it."

"What time of the night or morning was it?"

"Around three o'clock. I wouldn't have noticed, but nothing else moved on the street shot until that car went by." She tilted her head. "I'm still trying to figure out who he was visiting around here." The bell over the door rang and Janice looked past Riley and Mack to the newcomer. "Rocky. I've got your quarts of oil you asked me to order." She glanced again at Riley. "Don't be a stranger. It gets boring around here, and I love to visit."

"Yes, ma'am. We'll be back." Mack cupped Riley's elbow and led her out of the store.

"Do you think it was him?" Riley asked as soon as the door closed behind her.

Mack pulled his cell phone from his pocket and pressed Declan's number.

"Yo, Mack. What's up?"

"Sorry to bother you on vacation, but I could use some contacts."

"For what?"

"I need to run a license plate and find out who it belongs to."

"I can help you with that," Declan assured him. "Charlie gave me some names in the DC police department and a contact her husband had with the FBI. I'm sure one of them will be able to help."

Mack gave him the license plate of the dark-haired man and added, "It's urgent that we find out whose car it is as soon as possible. I'll fill you in later. I might need the team's help."

"On it. I'll get back with you as soon as I hear anything." Declan rang off.

"What can your team help with if we don't find our guy?" Riley asked.

"We're going to find him," Mack said, his jaw hardening. "And when we do, we'll need help extracting the boy. I'm sure they won't just hand him over." He anticipated a fight and hoped the boy wasn't collateral damage. "Right now we're getting breakfast at the local diner."

RILEY DIDN'T WANT to waste time eating when the minutes and hours were ticking by so quickly and they still hadn't found Toby. But she knew she couldn't operate without fuel for her body. What good would she be if she didn't have the energy to fight for her little brother?

Mack drove his truck to the diner and parked.

Before she could alight, he was there opening her door for her. She liked the gesture, but she didn't want to get used to it. Having been an independent woman all her life, she found it difficult letting a man treat her like the weaker sex. Especially knowing she very well could take him down in a few of the moves her father had taught her.

Her body heated at the thought of tossing Mack to the ground and pinning him between her thighs. He'd put up a fight, but she'd hold him there until he begged for mercy.

Or kissed her.

Her lips tingled at the memory of his previous kisses. She wanted more but didn't know quite how to ask for them. With her brother still unaccounted for and her handler possibly watching her every move, or that of Mrs. Halverson, she couldn't let her focus divert.

They entered the diner and chose a booth in a far corner.

"Hi, I'm Maddie. I'll be your server." A waitress with long, straight blond hair pulled back in a ponytail stopped beside Mack. "Our special this morning is two eggs any way you like them, bacon, hash browns and toast."

"I'll have the special," Mack said.

"Me, too," Riley echoed, her stomach rumbling loudly. When she thought back over the past three days, she hadn't had more than one meal since getting that message from Toby's abductor. She didn't feel right eating when Toby might not have been fed.

Mack reached across the table and covered her

hand with his. "You have to keep your strength up to help Toby. When the time comes, we might have to fight our way in and out to get to him. You can't do that without fueling your body."

Riley nodded. "I know. I just can't help wondering if Toby is being taken care of. I hope they're feeding him. The boy can pack away some groceries. He's growing again."

The waitress returned with glasses of water and orange juice. "You two are new in town, aren't you?" Her brow dipped as she studied Riley. "Though I think I've see you before."

Riley nodded. "I come occasionally."

"That's right." Maddie smiled. "You come in once or twice a month with Toby. He's such a good little boy. He's polite and well-mannered."

"Thank you. I'm proud of him." Considering what all he'd gone through, having lost his parents when he was a baby and living with his nanny and the occasional visit from his sister, he was growing up to be a very well-behaved young man.

"Will Toby be joining you?" Maddie asked.

"Not today," Riley answered.

Maddie left the table and returned a moment later with a coffee mug for each of them and a pot of coffee. "What brings you to Havenwood? Well, besides Toby."

"Actually, we were trying to track down a man

who might have come through here a couple days ago," Riley said. "I believe I left something in the rental car he's driving, and I want to retrieve it."

Mack thought Riley's story was a little weak, but the waitress seemed to buy it.

"Oh yeah?" Maddie tipped her head. "What does the car look like? Chances are I've see it."

"A silver four-door Prius sedan."

Maddie smiled. "Dark and four-door describes a lot of vehicles that come through the parking lot. Got anything more than that?"

"It has the license plate WMD 495."

"Oh, that car." Maddie snorted. "If it weren't for the license plate, I wouldn't have remembered that one. But WMD makes me think, *what would Mother do?*" She laughed. "My mother wouldn't be working in the diner, that's for sure. The man in the silver sedan pulled up in the parking lot like he was going to come in for something to eat. But he sat in the vehicle, facing the road, and then left a few minutes later. I thought maybe he was talking on his cell phone or something." She shrugged. "We were slow at that time. I could have used the tips. But whatever."

"Oh, well. I guess I'll keep looking," Riley said.

"I'd go back to the rental car company and see if they recovered your item," Maddie suggested.

"You're right," Riley said. "I'll do that."

Maddie disappeared into the kitchen and came back a few minutes later with their plates of food. "Can I get you anything else?"

"I don't need anything." Mack glanced toward Riley.

Riley shook her head. "Looks we have it all here. Thank you."

Once Maddie left them alone, Riley stabbed her fork into the eggs. "What do you think our mystery man was doing in the parking lot?"

"If he was facing the road, he might have been watching for Margaret and Toby to pass by."

"And then followed them out to the cabin." Riley's stomach roiled. But she shoveled food into her mouth, determined to be ready when the time came to fight for Toby's return. "We really need to know who owns that car."

Mack's phone vibrated on the tabletop. He glanced down at the screen. "It's Declan. Maybe he's got something for us to go on."

Riley leaned forward, her gaze on the phone. "I hope so. Answer it."

Mack already had his finger on the button to answer when she urged him to respond.

"Mack here," he said, and then listened in silence. "Okay. Send it to me in a text. We'll follow up." He ended the call and met Riley's gaze.

Her heart fluttered in her chest. "Well?"

"He got a hit. The car was rented by an Alan Durgan. He lives in Arlington. Declan is sending me his address."

Riley started to rise. "What are we waiting for? Let's go find him."

"Finish your food, and then we'll go."

"I'm full," Riley lied. Though she wasn't full, she couldn't eat another bite when her stomach twisted and churned.

"I need energy. I'm finishing, and then we'll leave." He touched her hand. "I'll hurry."

Riley sat across the table, trying to contain her impatience as Mack shoved his eggs and hash browns down his throat.

She even ate a few more bites as she waited. Less than five minutes later, Mack washed the food down with coffee, threw some bills on the table and stood. "Let's go."

Riley leaped to her feet and hurried out the door in front of Mack.

Once they were in the truck, she had to contain her excitement for the long drive back into the city. Since it was a weekend, the traffic wasn't as horrible as a workday, but it was steady and thick.

Riley cursed how slow the traffic moved. Finally, they reached their turnoff. Her heart beat faster as they neared the street address. They pulled into an apartment complex with peeling paint on the walls and run-down cars parked in the lot.

"Maybe you should stay here," Mack suggested.

Riley raised her eyebrows. "Really? I don't think so."

"Suit yourself. Just be ready. I don't have a good feeling about the neighborhood."

Three men in old jeans and faded shirts sat on the steps leading up to the building, smoking cigarettes.

Mack walked up to them.

Despite her bravado, Riley wasn't excited about passing the gauntlet of men in ragged clothing and smoke. But if the man inside the building had Toby, she'd do anything to get him out. Throwing back her shoulders, she followed Mack up the stairs, giving the men on the steps as much room as possible.

When she thought she'd made it past without incident, a hand reached out and gripped her ankle. Instinct took over. She turned the leg he held on to and shoved with all her might. The man fell off the steps backward, losing his grip on her ankle as he tumbled.

The other two men laughed at their friend.

Riley hurried up the steps after Mack before the man on the ground could recover.

Once inside, they climbed to the third floor and walked down a hallway that smelled like a dirty locker room to the fourth door on the left.

Mack raised his hand to knock. When his knuckles touched the door, it swung inward. The lock had been broken, and the doorframe was splintered.

Riley's heart plunged into her belly. She pushed past Mack and ran into the apartment, calling out, "Toby? Toby!"

No answer.

A moan came from a room to the right.

Riley started to enter, but Mack grabbed her arm and held her back. He pulled his handgun from beneath his jacket and waved her to the side.

Because he was armed, she let him take the lead, though it cost her to wait.

"Riley," Mack called out.

She ran into a bedroom containing a bare mattress and bloodstains on the wall.

Mack knelt on the far side of the bed. "We found our mystery man, but he's in bad shape."

Riley ran around the bed and stared down at a man with a hole in his chest, lying in a pool of blood. He reached up to clasp Mack's hand. Mack took it and held on as if he could keep the guy from dying by the strength of his grip.

"Where's the boy?" Mack demanded.

The man opened his mouth and coughed, and blood trickled from the corner of his lips. "He paid... me..." He coughed again, his chest rattling with fluid. "Paid me...to follow."

"Alan, who paid you?" Riley asked. "Does he have the boy? Did he take Toby?"

The man's gaze shifted to Riley. "Yes."

"Who is he? Please, tell me," Riley begged.

"Cash deal." Durgan coughed and closed his eyes.

"Alan Durgan, don't you die on me," Riley said. "That's my brother he has. Where did he take him?"

"Didn't know," Durgan whispered.

"Can you tell us anything about him?" Tears filled Riley's eyes and spilled down her cheeks. The man was going to die without telling them who had Toby.

"Badge. Had a badge."

"What kind of badge? Was he a police officer?"

"No. Worker badge…dropped when…paid." Durgan coughed, the rattle in his chest worse.

"Did the badge say where he worked?"

The man lay with his eyes closed, his breathing fading. He gasped, drawing in a rattling breath and letting it out with one word Riley could barely hear: "Quest."

"What did he look like? What was his name?" Riley grabbed the man's collar and shook him. "Don't die on me. Toby is all the family I have left."

Durgan didn't respond. He lay still, his chest no longer rattling, rising or anything. The man was dead, and with him went the knowledge of who had Toby.

Chapter Six

Mack placed the call to the police. While they waited for the authorities to arrive, they left the apartment and descended the stairs to the ground level.

Of the three men who'd been there when they came in, only one was left. The one Riley had shoved onto the ground. And he didn't look all too happy.

Mack lifted his chin and stared at the man, studying the tattoos on his arms. One stood out from the rest. "That's a Marine Corps emblem on your arm. You earn that or pay for it?" he asked.

"Both. Seven years, two deployments to the sandbox and a bum knee." The man's eyes narrowed. "What's it to you?"

"Did twelve in the corps." He held out his hand.

For a moment, the man stared at the hand. Then he took it and pulled Mack into a quick hug. "Thank you for your service, man."

"And you yours," Mack responded. "Name's Mack Balkman."

"Joe Sarly," the man introduced himself. "Who's your girlfriend?"

Riley started to open her mouth, but Mack answered before she could. "Riley."

Joe snorted. "Got a helluva kick." He nodded to Riley. "I deserved it."

"Damn right you did." Riley glared at the man.

He rubbed his chest and grinned. "You looked like a woman on a mission. I couldn't resist poking at you." He glanced up at the apartment building. "Who ya visiting?"

"Alan Durgan," Mack said.

Joe frowned. "The PI?"

"PI?" Riley asked.

"Yeah, he's a private investigator. Most of the time he's taking photos of men cheating on their wives or wives cheating on their husbands. What's he done to you?"

"He provided information to a man who kidnapped a child."

Joe's eyes widened. "No kidding? The dirtbag deserves to be shot."

"He got what he deserved," Riley muttered.

Joe looked at the building again. "What do you mean?"

"Someone shot him." Mack turned toward the

sound of the sirens wailing a couple of streets over. "The police will be here shortly."

Joe shifted on his feet, his gaze on the entrance to the parking lot. "Damn. I didn't really mean it about him deserving to be shot."

"How long have you been sitting on these steps?" Mack asked.

Joe shrugged. "A couple of hours."

"Did you see anyone besides us go into the apartment building during that time?"

"The lady who lives on the second floor came and went." Joe scratched his head. "And some guy delivered a package to one of the units inside."

"Do you know which floor?"

"I didn't follow him, if that's what you mean. But I could hear his footsteps for what sounded like a couple of flights of stairs." Joe's eyes got rounder. "You think the delivery guy offed Durgan?"

"We don't know, but I'm sure the police will want to ask the same questions." Mack nodded to the police car pulling into the parking lot.

As much as Mack didn't want to stick around and answer questions, he felt that if they left without speaking with the police, they'd appear guilty.

An hour later, Riley was pacing the parking lot, ready to leave. Declan managed to contact one of Charlie's contacts in the police department who cleared the way for them to leave as long as they dropped by the next day to sign a deposition about what they'd found in Durgan's apartment.

Mack held the door for Riley to climb into his truck. When she was settled in the seat, he rounded the hood and slipped into the driver's seat. They were on their way soon, weaving between the emergency vehicles that had gathered in response to Durgan's murder.

"The guy who has Toby works at Quest," Riley said, staring out the windshield, her fingers digging into the armrest so hard her knuckles turned white.

"We don't know that. He might have stolen a badge to get inside and spy on you."

"When badges are stolen, they don't go long before they are reported. The only reason he'd still have that badge is if he is on the inside."

"Do you think this has something to do with what happened a couple of weeks ago?" Mack asked. "Do you think the people who were stealing the secret project plans are paying you and Charlie back for interfering?"

Riley stared across the cab at Mack. "If that's the case, he could be one of four thousand employees in that building. How do we narrow the search down to one man? And how do I do that before the weekend is over? Surely he'll want to know Mrs. Halverson died before Monday. He's expecting a quick death.

And if I didn't do it right, he might step in and finish the job."

"My guys will be watching over Charlie. They'll make sure he doesn't get anywhere near her."

"Can you be certain?"

He held up one hand, the other firmly on the steering wheel. "They can be trusted to protect her."

"But I got to her when you were supposed to be protecting her."

Mack's fingers tightened on the steering wheel. "I thought you were one of the good guys."

"And I thought I was, too." She stared down at her hands. "Sometimes we do things we don't want to do to protect those we love."

"I failed Charlie this time." He'd been surprised the widow had let him stay on with Declan's Defenders after he let her into the restroom with an assassin. "My guys won't let it happen again."

"I need to get inside Quest. Maybe the man who has Toby is connected with the folks who were stealing secrets."

"I thought the only one in Quest who was helping with that was your old supervisor. And he's dead."

"Yes, he is, but there might have been more."

"And how will you be able to single him out when most people are at home for the weekend?"

"I don't know. I just think the answer is at Quest."

"Can you get me in?"

She shook her head. "Not through the front door. Declan got in last time by sneaking in via a delivery truck."

"The chances of that happening on a weekend are slim to none."

"Then I'll have to go alone."

"What about the cleaning crew? Does Quest have a service?"

Riley's eyes narrowed. "Yes. They come in after hours and on weekends when there aren't many people in the building. I remember working on a Saturday and Sunday and hearing the sound of the vacuum cleaner on my floor."

"All I have to do is slip in when they do."

"There are security cameras throughout the building."

"Then I have to look like I'm cleaning. Easy enough."

Riley's brow wrinkled. "You hardly look like the cleaning crew."

"I can disguise myself. You can get in on your own ID and I'll find a way in via the cleaning crew."

"Okay." Riley nodded and focused on the road ahead. "Then what?"

"We track down who your supervisor had contact with. You might also check your desk for bugs and your computer for Trojan horses. Someone might have a backdoor into your computer at work who is monitoring your communications."

Riley shook her head. "I'm very careful about changing my passwords."

"If there's a listening device or camcorder recording your movements, it doesn't matter how many times you change your password. Someone could be recording your changes as you make them." Mack brushed her arm with the backs of his knuckles. "You could be doing the right things and still be giving away secrets."

"Damn." She ran a hand through her hair. "If he wants the data I kept him from getting, why ask me to kill Charlie?"

"Apparently, he knows Charlie was behind the foiled attempt to secure the data. That and if you killed Charlie, he had that over you to make you do whatever he wanted. All he had to do was threaten to expose you."

"And use Toby as his leverage if that didn't work." Riley closed her eyes. "He has no intention of giving Toby back to me."

"Which makes it all the more imperative we find the child and get him back."

Riley nodded and bit her bottom lip. "That poor kid has to be traumatized by all this. He can't help who his parents were and who his sister is. Why can't they leave him alone?"

"Because they know he's your weakness," Mack reminded her. He reached for her hand and held it. "But if you're going to have a weakness, it's a good one to have. It shows you have a heart."

She tightened her fingers around his and held his hand the rest of the way to the building where she worked.

Mack liked the way her fingers felt, supple but strong. He could imagine how they'd feel sweeping across his naked chest and lower. He admired her strength and her commitment to her brother. If he'd had a chance to save his brother, he'd have taken it. He knew how it felt to lose someone you love, especially someone who had his entire life ahead of him. Aiden had barely begun to live. Mack refused to let anything happen to Toby. That kid was like the little brother Mack had lost all those years ago. They had to find him. He had to live. For Riley. For Aiden.

RILEY STARED THROUGH the windshield at the street ahead, her mind going through all the possibilities. Who at Quest had been watching her besides her supervisor? Who would have paid a PI to follow Toby and the nanny? Who had bugged her apartment?

All those questions remained unanswered as long

as she sat in Mack's truck. She needed action, and she felt that she'd find the answers at Quest.

When they approached the building, Riley had Mack circle the block. A van stood at the rear of the building near the loading dock. The writing on the van indicated it was from the cleaning agency that serviced the building.

Three women left the Quest building, walked to the van and climbed inside. They pulled out of the dock area and drove out onto the street.

"Follow them," Riley said. She glanced at her watch. "It's noon. They might be going out to get something to eat."

Mack gave the van a sufficient lead before he turned onto the street behind them.

After several turns, the van stopped at a pizzeria and the three women entered the establishment.

Mack pulled into a parking lot at the Thai restaurant one building over from the pizzeria. "Be ready to roll. I'll be right back." He opened the driver's door and dropped down from the truck.

Riley slid across the console into the driver's seat, her heart pounding. "Where are you going?"

"Into that van."

She waved toward the vehicle in question. "But it's out in the open."

"If those women are hungry, they aren't watching the van. They're watching the guys inside making pizza." He walked across the parking lot as if he were going to pass the back of the van. As he came abreast of the back door, he tried the handle. The door swung open and Mack disappeared inside.

Riley held her breath, her gaze going from the van to the pizzeria. What if the ladies came out early? What if they caught Mack in the back of the van? Would they call the police?

A moment later, the door of the pizzeria opened and the three women came out carrying two boxes each of pizzas. They were laughing and smiling as they walked toward the van.

One entered through the sliding side door at the same time the back door opened and Mack slipped out, carrying a bundle. He eased the door closed and hunkered low, waiting for the side door to close and the other two women to get into the van.

Then he made his move, walking out from behind the van as if he were passing by. Only he walked away from where Riley sat in the truck.

The ladies in the van pulled away from the pizzeria and back out onto the street.

Riley whipped the truck into Drive and went around the other side of the pizza place, where Mack stood with his bundle, grinning.

"What did you do?" Riley asked as he jumped into the passenger seat and slammed the door closed.

"I got my ticket into Quest." He held up a security badge and a jumpsuit with the name of the cleaning company embroidered on the front along with a woman's name. Eudora.

"You're going into Quest dressed as a cleaning lady?"

He nodded. "I am. Didn't Declan get in as a package delivery guy? I figure if he can do it, so can I."

"One big drawback." Riley stared at the badge and at Mack. "You don't look anything like Eudora."

"I'll wear a baseball cap."

Riley shook her head. The idea of the big marine dressing up as a cleaning lady was ludicrous. "You think you'll fit in that jumpsuit?"

He nodded. "It's big."

"Yeah, but you're tall. That thing will barely go past your knees."

He slipped out of his shoes and shoved his feet into the legs of the jumpsuit. "It'll do to get me past the gate and the security cameras."

"And if it doesn't?"

"Then I'll run like hell and come up with another idea. At the very least, you'll get through the door and I'll provide a little distraction while you poke around your office."

Riley drew in a deep breath and pressed her foot

to the accelerator. "You're crazy, Mack Balkman. You know that, don't you?"

"We do what we have to do to get the job done." He shoved his arms into the sleeves and dragged the jumpsuit up over his broad shoulders. As he said, the jumpsuit was very large. Eudora must be a big woman.

Even so, he had to strain to get the front zipper all the way up. The fabric stretched taut over his muscles, and the legs of the suit didn't cover his ankles. Thankfully, his boots covered the rest.

"You could do with a shave," Riley muttered. "Unless Eudora is also prone to facial hair."

"I've got that covered." Mack reached in the glove box and pulled out a battery-powered razor. Moments later he'd removed most of the stubble from his chin, neck and cheeks.

Riley reached into her purse with one hand and rummaged around until she found a tube of lipstick. "Use this. It can't hurt."

Mack made a face but uncapped the lipstick and pulled the visor down to look at his reflection in the mirror. With an unpracticed hand, he applied a coat of fire-engine red to his lips and rubbed them together. When he was done, he clapped a cap on his head and grinned.

Riley laughed out loud. "For such a good-looking guy, you're an ugly woman."

"But will I do?"

Riley studied him briefly before returning her attention to the street. "You'll do." She gave him the location of her office. "I'll watch for you and let you in when you get there. Only authorized personnel are allowed back there, but I know some of the cleaning staff have been cleared to enter for house-keeping purposes only."

Mack glanced down at his name tag. "Hopefully, Eudora was one of them."

Riley's lips curled for the rest of the drive to the Quest campus. Mack dressed as a cleaning lady was too funny to not see the humor in the situation. She wished she could take the time to snap a picture of him. His buddies would give him hell.

Two blocks from the building, Riley pulled into an empty parking lot, parked the truck and nodded to Mack. "I'll go first."

"I won't be long behind you."

"*If* you get in."

"I'll get in," he said, smiling with his bright red lipstick. "Just watch." Then he winked.

Riley got out of the truck, clipped her badge on her shirt and slipped her purse over her shoulder. The way she saw it, her time was running out. If she didn't find something inside the walls of Quest, she didn't know where she'd look next, or if she had time.

Hang in there, Toby. I'm trying.

Chapter Seven

Mack waited until Riley entered the gate at Quest before he left the truck and made his way to the same gate. He checked his stride, hoping to imitate the way Riley walked with the natural sway of her hips and the much shorter steps. He had to look ridiculous in the jumpsuit that was too short and too tight. But it didn't matter as long as he got through the gate using Eudora's badge. Once inside, he'd find his way up to the floor where Riley worked.

Hunching over a little, he tried to make himself as small and short as possible, which was hard to do for a man over six feet tall. At the gate, he slid the badge through the card reader and waited for the light to turn green and the gate lock to click. For a second, he thought the card wasn't going to work, but then the light flickered to green. He pushed through quickly and strode across the campus to the entrance.

As he passed the guard at the front desk, he averted his gaze and hurried toward the elevators.

"Hey!"

Out of Mack's peripheral vision, he noticed the guard rising from his desk.

Pretending he didn't hear, Mack punched the button for the elevator going up and counted his heartbeats until the door slid open.

"Hey, you!" the guard called out again.

"George, what are you doing on Saturday shift?" a female voice called out.

"Hey, Lois, long time no see," George said, his voice not nearly as loud.

The elevator doors slid open. Mack stepped in and turned to punch the button for the floor where Riley worked. Then he hit the button to close the elevator door. He glanced across the floor to where George stood talking to Lois.

George looked over Lois's shoulder at Mack. For a moment, the guard's eyes narrowed.

Then the elevator door closed, and the car moved upward.

Mack let out the breath he'd been holding, willed his pulse to slow to normal and watched the floor numbers blink on and off until he stopped at Riley's floor.

The door opened, and Mack stepped out.

Just outside the elevator stood a cleaning cart.

Mack looked both ways but didn't see a cleaning person. He grabbed the handle of the cart and pushed it down the hallway toward the sign over the door that read Special Projects.

As he reached the door, it opened.

For a split second, Mack froze.

Then Riley poked her head out and waved him toward her. "In here."

Mack pushed the cart through the door.

Riley closed it behind him.

"Remember to look for bugs or hidden cameras," he whispered to her.

She nodded and held up a small electronic device that had been smashed. "Found this attached inside the receiver of my desk phone."

"I'll dust my way around the overhead light fixtures and see what I can clean out."

"Good. In the meantime, I'll be working my way through my desktop computer."

Their conversation was whispered. Riley barely moved her lips as she spoke.

Mack wanted to bend down and kiss those incredibly pretty lips he knew to be soft and pliable beneath his. Then he recalled how ridiculous he looked and wondered if a woman like Riley would ever want to kiss him after seeing him dressed as he was, wearing red lipstick.

"By the way…" Riley glanced up, a wicked gleam

in her eyes. "You're cute in that getup." Before he could respond, she turned and walked away.

Pushing the cart in front of him, Mack followed Riley into the realm of the Special Projects unit. He unloaded the small vacuum cleaner from the cart and plugged it into an electric socket. Then working his way from one end of the aisle Riley had gone down to the other, he vacuumed and dusted, checking the overhead light fixtures as he went. At one point, he climbed onto a stepladder he found affixed to the side of the cleaning cart to dust the fluorescent light that illuminated Riley's desk. Inside the fixture he found a small device the size of a single throwing die. He swept the duster across it and trapped it in the microfiber, then dropped it into a trash bin, covering it with a wad of paper towels.

Riley barely acknowledged him. She worked at her computer, her head bent toward the screen, her fingers flying across the keyboard.

Mack emptied trash bins from beneath each of the desks surrounding Riley's, checking through the discarded papers. He looked at the items on the desks, photographs and notes, hoping to find some anomaly. Most of the desks had photographs of family members or pets. Except one. The nameplate on the wall outside the cubicle read Steve Pruett.

Mack committed the name to memory. He'd ask

Riley about Pruett when they were out of the building and somewhere it was safe to talk.

Dusting his way down the aisle on the far side of Riley's cubicle, Mack paused when he thought he heard the door to the area creak open.

"Hello?" a female voice called out.

Mack ducked low and moved toward the end of the corridor to get a better view of the person who'd just entered.

Riley poked her head above the five-foot-high walls of the cubes and answered, "Can I help you?"

"Sorry to disturb you, ma'am, but I seem to have misplaced my cleaning cart. I don't suppose you've seen one around here?"

"Bridgett, is that you?"

"Oh, hi, Miss Lansing. Why are you here working on a weekend?"

"I had some catching up to do, since I was out a few days," Riley responded. "I haven't seen your cleaning cart, but then I haven't been looking for one. Have you tried the area on the other side of the hall?"

"I have. It wasn't there. I went down to supply for some window cleaner, came back and the cart was gone. Do you mind if I look?"

"No," Riley said. "Go for it."

Great. Mack listened for the sound of footsteps, gauged the direction they were coming from and went the opposite.

Just as he slipped around the end of the row of cubicles, he heard a gasp.

"Ah, there it is," the cleaning woman said.

"You find it?" Riley asked.

"I did. I don't know how it got in here, but it's okay. I'll get out of your hair and come back later to clean this area."

"Thank you," Riley said.

Mack hid in a cubicle on the other side of the wall from where he'd left the cleaning cart. He carefully controlled his breathing so the member of the cleaning staff didn't hear him or come around the end of the row to find him lurking in his borrowed jumpsuit, with his purloined badge and red lipstick.

The cleaning woman wheeled the cart out of Special Projects, closing the door behind her.

Mack waited a full minute before he worked his way back to where Riley worked.

"That was close," Riley said. "Find anything?"

"Other than the camcorder in your light fixture... no."

"Camcorder?" Riley shivered. "I can't believe that even in this area, someone was able to get in, plant devices and get out without being noticed."

"Have you found anything?"

"I was able to get into the shared drives and into my old supervisor's stored emails. He wrote some cryptic emails to one of the department heads that made no sense."

"The emails or the department head?"

Riley's lips twitched. "The emails."

"That department head ever act weird around you?"

Her brow wrinkled. "I don't think so. Though I don't think Bryan Young liked me much. He always had a scowl on his face like he'd eaten something that didn't agree with him."

"When you were trying to figure out who was selling secrets, was Young ever on your list of maybes?" Mack asked.

Riley lifted a shoulder. "I guess he was. But my contacts with the FBI never found anything on him."

"Who else were they monitoring?"

"Mr. Moretti, my supervisor, and Tracy Gibson, his secretary."

"What happened to Tracy when Mr. Moretti didn't come back to work?" Mack asked.

"She was laid off. No one wanted to take her on, knowing Mr. Moretti was one of the insiders helping to sell secrets."

"Do you think she was as dirty as Moretti?"

"Hard to say. She might only have been in the wrong job with the wrong boss."

Mack stared down at her. "What does your gut say?"

"After Moretti showed his true colors, I wouldn't have trusted her."

"She bears looking into. Whoever has Toby wanted Charlie dead. The rich widow could have been targeted for a number of reasons, one of which was hiring Declan to help find you, and in the process, exposing Moretti and the leak inside Quest."

"Do you think they want Charlie dead out of vengeance?"

"It's as good a motivation as any. And since you were involved in setting up the sting, what better way to dispose of Charlie than to force you to do it? And then you would be exposed for the Russian sleeper spy you were trained to be."

"Could my handler be that entrenched in Quest and possibly one of the traitors selling or even buying the secrets?" Riley shook her head. "There are too many coincidences. And if the person on the inside of Quest isn't actually my handler, how did he know the code word for my activation?"

"All good questions we won't know the answers to until we find Toby and his kidnapper."

"Then we better get started. I say we follow Bryan Young and see what he might know."

"Got an address?" Mack asked.

"I was able to hack into HR files." Riley pulled a sheet of paper off a pad and stuffed it into her pocket. "Got it."

"Get Tracy Gibson's, too," Mack insisted.

"Give me a second." Riley clicked keys and leaned toward the monitor.

"And while you're at it, Steve Pruett," Mack added.

She glanced up, her brow wrinkling. "Steve? Why him?"

"Just in case. His was the only desk with nothing on it."

"Steve tends to be overly particular about his things. I'm not surprised his desk is neat. But a Russian spy?" Riley shook her head.

"He's too neat. No indication of who he is. No personality, makes me think of a sociopath, in my opinion."

Riley brought up Steve's information and jotted down his address. "Got him and Tracy. Anyone else?"

"I didn't see any other desk that triggered my instincts."

Riley pursed her lips. "It's sad when all we have to go on is gut instinct."

"And your digging in the HR files."

"I hope they can't trace back to my hacking."

"If Quest learns of your Russian upbringing, do you think they'd let you continue to work for them?"

Riley sighed. "I don't think any American company would let me work for them."

"Then let's go." Riley pushed herself to her feet.

The door to the Special Projects unit opened at the same time. She ducked low. "Wait, someone's coming," she whispered."

Mack dived into a cubicle and crouched behind a file cabinet. He didn't like that he couldn't confront whoever had come in, but he was the odd man in the room. Riley was the one who belonged.

RILEY SAT BACK at her desk and pulled up one of the drawings she'd been working on before everything had gone south in her life.

The tall, angular form of the head of the department, Bryan Young, stopped beside her desk. "Miss Lansing. I'm surprised to see you working on a weekend."

She glanced up with a forced smile. "Oh, Mr. Young, I could say the same about you."

The department head frowned. "I'm here quite often on Saturdays, or I wouldn't have made that remark."

"Oh, well… I was out a couple days and my work fell behind. I thought I'd come in and try to catch up. But I was just finishing what I was doing, and I'm about to leave. I have a few errands to run before I head home." She exited out of the drawing file and pushed to her feet. "Are you staying long?"

The man shook his head. "No. I just stopped by to check on a few things and collect a document I needed to read over before Monday. Then I'm out of here."

"Good. Weekends are for family," Riley said. Normally, she'd be out at the cabin, spending time with Toby. Her heart squeezed hard in her chest at the thought of her little brother. She prayed they didn't hurt him.

The man snorted. "Or a long to-do list," Young muttered. "Have a nice day, Miss Lansing."

"Thank you, Mr. Young. You, too." She gathered her purse and stepped around the department head.

"Oh, and Miss Lansing, Human Resources has decided to conduct a thorough rescreening of all employees since Mr. Moretti's untimely death and the ugly business of selling secrets to foreign countries. The FBI has asked to be involved." Young gave her a narrow-eyed glance. "I trust that you weren't involved in Moretti's dealings."

Riley tensed. "I assure you, Mr. Young, I had nothing to do with selling secrets to anyone. I work for Quest only." She could say that with truth in her heart. Though she worked with the FBI to help flush out all those involved in selling data and plans from the project she had been working on, Riley had given bad data for the transfers to keep the data thieves from getting the real data for the secret project. None of her hard work had made it into the wrong hands, unless Moretti had hacked into her files and passed on the information before he was shot and killed.

"Well, I'm done here," Riley said. "See you Monday." If she found her brother, and if she still had a job then.

Riley walked toward the exit door, her pulse racing. Where was Mack? She prayed Mr. Young didn't decide to inspect every desk in the Special Projects unit.

Mack needed Young to leave the area so that he could get out without being seen.

Riley waited until Young was almost to his office before she hurried after him. "Mr. Young. I had a question for you about Mr. Moretti's replacement."

She made it a point to pass by the cubicle where Mack hid. As she passed him, she jerked her thumb toward the exit.

"What is your question, Miss Lansing?"

"Are you going outside the organization to replace him, or will you be promoting within?" She stopped beside the man where he paused with his hand on the doorknob to his office.

He twisted the knob and pushed the door inward. "Why do you ask, Miss Lansing?" The man stepped through the door.

Riley glanced back over her shoulder.

A shadowy movement assured her Mack was

making his way to the exit. All Riley had to do was divert Young's attention until Mack cleared the unit.

"Mr. Young, I've been with Quest for over five years and moved up in ranks each year. I believe I could be the supervisor over Special Projects. I know everyone on the team and the work that is being done."

"I'll be sure to keep your name in mind when we decide to advertise the position."

Out of the corner of her eye, Riley saw the exit door open and close.

"Thank you, Mr. Young. I just want you to know I'm interested in the position. Have a good day."

"Same to you, Miss Lansing." Already, the man's attention had shifted to the contents of his desktop.

Riley backed out of the office and turned to leave.

She had just reached the door leading out of the unit when she noticed Mr. Young leaving his office and locking the door behind him.

The man hadn't stayed long and seemed to be in a hurry to get somewhere.

Riley had no desire to share an elevator with the man. When she stepped out into the hallway, she looked for Mack. He was nowhere to be seen. Instead of taking the elevator, Riley took the stairs down to the ground floor. When she exited the stairwell, she sought out Mack in his costume, but still didn't see him.

Hoping Mack had found his way out of the building, Riley left Quest and its campus and found her way back to the truck a couple blocks away.

Mack sat in the driver's seat, scrubbing the lipstick off his mouth with a napkin. He'd removed the jumpsuit and cap and looked more like himself.

"Did Young give you the job?" Mack asked.

Riley snorted. "I don't think it's completely up to him. The job will have to be advertised and posted so others can apply. They have to go through the motions, even if they have someone in mind for the position." She stared out at a vehicle leaving the Quest campus. "That should be Mr. Young. Now would be a good time to follow him."

"Did you get a feeling from him that he might have Toby?"

"I didn't, but why would Moretti have sent those memos to him in some kind of code?"

"I don't know, but let's follow him and find out what he's up to."

With his lips still brighter red than he liked, Mack pulled out onto the street and fell in behind Bryan Young, staying back far enough the man wouldn't be suspicious.

Young drove for twenty minutes, working his way out of town heading west into the countryside.

Riley sat forward in her seat, her eyes glued to

the expensive car in front of her. "Do you think he has Toby?"

Mack didn't say it, but his gut wasn't feeling it. "I don't know." And if they spent too much time chasing Young and he turned out to be the wrong man, they'd have wasted time they could be using to go after someone else. Mack pulled out his cell phone. "Call Gus. Ask him how Charlie's doing."

Riley found the right number and hit the call button.

"Hey, Mack," Gus answered, his voice coming over the truck's sound system. "How's the hunt for the little boy going?"

"Not well. We don't have a lot to go on."

"Sorry to hear that. We've had a little excitement here at the hospital."

"What's happening?"

"Someone dressed as a nurse tried to slip past us in the middle of the night to get to Charlie."

Mack's fingers tightened around the steering wheel. "How's Charlie?"

"Fine. Getting a little antsy. But she's fine. Mustang wouldn't let anyone into Charlie's room. Not even the doctor on call. Charlie pulled some strings and has her personal physician checking in on her."

"Did you run a check on the nurse who tried to get in?"

"Mustang had the sense to snap a picture of the

badge. We ran it against the hospital employees' database. That nurse reported a missing badge this morning."

"Were you able to detain the woman?" Mack asked.

"No, she left as soon as Mustang snapped a photo of her badge. Mustang wouldn't leave his post to follow her, and I was on a coffee run. By the time I got word, the woman was gone."

"Have Mustang send that photo of her badge and hopefully of the woman to me and Declan."

"Already sent to Declan. He passed it on to one of Charlie's contacts with face recognition software."

"Great."

"Snow and McCastlain are doubling up on shift. If anyone tries again, we'll have backup."

"Glad to hear it," Mack said. "Keep Charlie safe."

"We've got her covered," Gus said. "Question is, do you need help?"

"I've got Declan chasing down some leads via Charlie's contacts. Riley and I are following a lead now. Hopefully something will turn up. In the meantime, we're working against the clock. I fully expect Riley to get a phone call soon if Charlie doesn't show up in the news as having passed."

"We'll do our best to keep that from happening, but that doesn't help Riley get her brother back."

"Exactly."

"Stay in contact."

"Will do," Mack said, and ended the call.

"Mr. Young just turned off," Riley said.

The car in front of them exited the main highway onto a side road.

Mack slowed the truck, giving Young enough time to pull ahead.

By the time Mack turned off the main highway, Young had made another turn and disappeared.

"Damn." Mack pressed his foot hard on the accelerator.

"There!" Riley pointed down a street to the right. "He just turned left two blocks down."

Mack drove another block and turned right, sped past one block and was well on the way to the second.

"Slow down." Riley leaned forward. "He stopped at a house on the next street. Stop the truck. We can walk from here without alerting him to the fact that he's being followed."

Mack pulled the truck to a stop against the curb and shifted into Park.

Riley was out of her seat and dropping to the ground before he could round the front of the truck. Together, they ran between buildings. Mack could see the car Young had been driving pull into the back alley behind a yellow-and-white cottage.

Riley slowed to a stop behind a bush and parted the branches. "He's going in through the back door.

He could have Toby in there." When she started to go around the bushes, he stopped her.

"Wait and let him get inside."

"But—"

"He could be visiting his mother for all we know," Mack reminded her.

As Young climbed the steps to the back porch, the back door opened, and a pretty woman with bleached-blond hair stepped out and flung her arms around Young's neck.

"I could be wrong, but that's not his mother," Riley said.

The woman wrapped her arms around Young's neck and kissed him.

"And I'd bet that's not his daughter."

"I've met his wife," Riley said. "That's not her."

Chapter Eight

Riley held back long enough for Mr. Young to get inside the house. Then she ducked around the bush and hurried toward the little yellow-and-white house. Apparently, her department head was having an affair. But did that make him a Russian spy? And did it mean he was the one holding Toby hostage? She doubted it, but they'd come this far; they had to be certain.

Mack caught up to her and got to the house before her.

Since he was taller, he could see in through the window without having to climb up onto the porch.

"See anything?"

"Just the two of them kissing."

"Any sign of Toby?"

"No." Mack moved from that window to another.

Riley followed. "And the windows aren't completely covered. You'd think if they had the boy, they'd have him hidden."

"You'd think if they were having an affair, they'd hide it better. Any private investigator could have a field day snapping photos."

Making a semicircle around the house, Mack checked every window. "From what I can tell, there isn't a basement. I'm not seeing any sign of anyone other than Young and the woman. And they only have eyes for each other."

"Give me a boost," Riley demanded.

Mack cupped his hands. "Have a look."

Riley stepped into his palms.

Mack raised her to eye level with the window.

As he'd mentioned, Mr. Young and the woman were heavy into kissing and more. Clothes were flying off, and Mr. Young backed the woman against the wall.

"Good Lord, that's Rachel from HR." Riley jerked and knocked her forehead against the glass pane.

The couple stopped in mid-grope and turned toward the window.

Riley dropped down, her heart pounding. "They might have seen me. We need to get out of here."

"You feel confident they don't have Toby?" Mack asked as they ran around a thick stand of bushes.

"Positive."

"If you think there might be a chance they have him hidden in a closet, I'll go knock on the door. They don't know me. I could make up some story to get them to let me in."

"No. I think we're wasting our time." Riley stood still for a moment, afraid to move unless Young and his lover caught sight of her.

The back door opened, and the woman peered out. Mr. Young stood in the shadows behind her.

Riley held her breath.

The woman shook her head and turned, closing the door behind her.

Riley grabbed Mack's hand. "Come on, we have to check out the other two people on our list. I feel like we're running out of time."

A dog barked as they passed a fence, and someone yelled for it to shut up.

Riley broke into a run, a sense of urgency making her pulse race and her stomach twist. Mack opened the door for her and then hurried around to get into the driver's seat.

"Where to next?" Mack shifted into Drive and pulled out onto the street.

"Steve Pruett's place." Riley stared down at the map function on her cell phone where she'd keyed in Steve's address. "It's about twenty minutes from here."

"We'll make it in fifteen." Mack pushed down hard on the accelerator.

Riley stared out the window, despair eating away at hope. "I feel like we're on a wild-goose chase."

Mack reached across and gathered Riley's hand in his. He gave it a gentle squeeze. "As long as Toby's out there, we can't give up hope."

She nodded, her heart swelling at Mack's touch. He gave her strength in the simple contact. "I'm not giving up," she assured him. "But there has to be a better way to find him than chasing down impossible leads."

As if on cue, Mack's cell phone rang.

Riley lifted it and read the caller ID screen. "Declan." She slid her finger across the display. "Hey, Declan. Tell me something good."

"We had a hit on Steve Pruett."

"What kind of hit?"

"We found a police report about a domestic disturbance at his house a month ago. The neighbor called it in. When they arrived, his girlfriend refused to press charges, even though she had a busted lip. She swore she'd walked into a door."

"That doesn't mean he's a kidnapper."

"No, but we also found information on a debt collection agency. The man owes over $100,000 in credit card bills. Apparently, he likes to live at a level greater than his salary warrants."

"Motivation to sell secrets, but not to kill," Riley said.

"Unless someone is paying him to have you do the killing," Declan suggested. "He bears looking into. Grace and I cut our vacation short. We're back at Charlie's place with the computer guy who worked with her late husband. He's an expert hacker. We've got him digging into anything to do with Pruett."

"Good. We're on our way to Pruett's address. Anything you find in the next twenty minutes could help."

"Will let you know. And we didn't find anything on Bryan Young. Other than his wife recently filed for divorce. They're in marriage counseling, to mediate and salvage their marriage."

"Yeah, that's not going to happen," Mack muttered.

Riley's lips twisted into a wry grin. "Anything on Tracy Gibson?"

"The most we could find was that she's drawing unemployment for now. No police record or rap sheet on her."

"So far, Pruett's all we have. If your hacker can get into Moretti's computer at Quest or his home, have him see what he can dig up."

"Will do," Declan said.

"We'll let you know what we find at Pruett's place." Mack ended the call with a touch to a button on the steering wheel. "What do you know about Steve Pruett?"

Riley shook her head. "That's just it. I don't know much about any of my coworkers. I was so busy working and spending time on the weekend with my brother. And when the FBI got me involved with finding the leak in our department, I was focused on Moretti. I didn't see anything in any of the others... because I wasn't looking." She clenched her hands into fists. "Too many secrets. I hate living a life of secrets. But how did Pruett find out about mine? No one knew but my parents' handler, as far as I know. Why would the handler share that information?"

"Unless he had an agenda of his own and needed to keep his identity secret."

Riley glanced down at the map on her phone. "We turn here. Two blocks over and turn to the right." Once again, her heart beat faster. If Pruett was their man, he could have Toby locked up in his house.

"Parking now."

Before he had the gearshift fully engaged in Park, she was out of the truck and running toward Pruett's address. Pruett had to be their guy. Toby could be yards away.

Riley's heart raced as her legs powered her forward.

A hand on her arm jerked her back.

"You can't go charging up to the house. He's not

just going to hand over Toby." Mack brought her up short at the corner of a house three doors down from the target address and gripped both her arms, forcing her to look at him. "We have to take it slowly."

Riley nodded. "I know. I know. I just…it's Toby. I have to get him back. He's bound to be scared to death."

"If he's there, we'll get him."

Riley curled her hands into his shirt. "He has to be there."

"We'll soon find out." He swept his hand along the side of her cheek and brushed a strand of her hair back behind her ear. Then he bent and touched his lips to hers. "Let's do this." Mack took the lead and slipped behind the houses, following an alley that paralleled the street out front.

Riley shifted her gaze from the buildings ahead to her cell phone, tracking their progress since they weren't looking at the numbers on the curb or mailboxes. "This is it," she said, stopping short of the house. The backyard was surrounded by a chain-link fence. The one before it had a collection of old junk stacked in varying piles. Not Pruett's house. The yard was pristine. Absent of everything but neatly trimmed grass. He didn't even have bushes around the foundation.

"He has a basement." Riley pointed to a trapdoor with a padlock securing the outside.

"Let's see if he's home." Mack inched up to one of the windows and peeked inside.

"See anything?"

"No movement."

Riley eased around the side of the building to the garage and looked through the window into a one-car garage. "No car. He must be out. We can get inside and be out before he returns."

"That's breaking and entering."

"I don't care if I have to smash a window. I'm going in." Riley dug in her jacket pocket for the file she kept handy for just such an occasion. She climbed the stairs to the back porch and slipped the file into the lock on the door. Within seconds, she had the door open.

"One of your spy skills?"

"My father had me tinkering with locks from a very early age," Riley admitted. "I'm good at it." As she crossed the threshold into Pruett's house, she glanced back. "Stay outside. I don't want you taking the rap for breaking and entering. It'll be all on me, if I get caught."

"You're not going in alone." Mack followed her up the stairs and entered the house, closing the door behind them.

The house was old, with hardwood floors, crisply painted walls and not a cobweb or dust bunny anywhere. The hallway passed a small laundry room.

Riley glanced through that doorway and moved on. Mack entered, checked it thoroughly and followed Riley into the kitchen.

A study in white, the kitchen was like the rest of the house, sparkling clean with white marble countertops and white cabinets with chrome pull handles, polished bright. No fingerprints marring the smooth finish.

Riley lifted her hands, afraid to touch anything for fear of leaving evidence that she'd been there. A staircase led off the kitchen up to the second floor. Riley hurried up the steps. Two bedrooms were completely empty with no furnishings or wall hangings. The light fixtures were clean, and cobwebs wouldn't dare make an appearance in the rooms.

Mack led the way back to the ground floor and found a door beneath the staircase. Using the hem of his T-shirt, he opened the door and flipped on the light switch. A light hung overhead but only illuminated the staircase, nothing beyond.

Mack went down first.

Riley held her breath and followed.

Once they reached the concrete floor below, they had to turn to see into the rest of the basement. A shiny steel toolbox stood in one corner next to a workbench. Behind the workbench was a pegboard with tools hanging neatly. Each tool had an outline on the pegboard. Every tool had a place and every tool was in it.

Riley had the sudden urge to knock them all down and fling them across the floor in disarray. None of the tools had any dings, dirt or oil on them. They appeared to be barely used.

Mack made a quick inspection of the rest of the basement. "Nothing here," he said.

"No secret doors?" Riley made her own pass through the room. "No hidden rooms?"

"Nothing."

Her heart sank. "Where's Toby?" she whispered.

"I don't know, but we need to get out of here before Pruett returns and catches us."

"Where would he keep a little boy?"

"We don't even know it's Pruett who has him."

"What about the girlfriend? Can your friend Declan find her?"

"I hope so. Let's get out of here. This place gives me the creeps."

"Me, too." Riley climbed the stairs and had reached out to push the door wider when she heard a sound that made her blood run cold. The front doorknob rattled.

"Someone's at the door." Riley eased back, switched off the light and pulled the door almost all the way closed. The only light came from the gap between the bottom of the door and the floor.

Riley stepped down a step and bent to look through the gap.

As she suspected, someone was coming through the front door. All she could see was a pair of men's leather shoes moving across the floor. The crisp *tap* of heels on wooden floors echoed off the walls.

The wearer of the shoes paused in the hallway. A rustle of fabric sounded, and a garment hit the floor. From what Riley could see, it was a jacket and was quickly snatched up.

The shoes moved toward the door behind which Riley and Mack stood.

Short of stumbling down the stairs in the dark, Riley could do nothing but freeze and pray the shoes didn't stop.

She held her breath and waited, fully expecting the door to burst open and Pruett to call the police. Bunching her muscles, she prepared to launch herself up out of the basement and run like hell. Though what good that would do, she didn't know. Pruett would recognize her, and she'd be charged with breaking and entering. What bothered her most was that Mack would be charged as well.

The shoes slowed on their way past the door but didn't stop.

Riley listened as the footsteps passed the kitchen and moved on to the bedroom on the main level. Moments later, the sound of water rushing through the pipes gave her hope.

"He's taking a shower." Mack touched her arm. "If we want to leave, now would be the time."

Riley eased the door open and stuck her head around the edge. The water rushing through the pipes suddenly stopped. Going out the back door would force them to pass the door to the main floor bedroom. Instead, Riley headed for the front door, opening it quietly and easing through the screen door.

Mack followed, closing the door carefully behind them.

Once she was out of the house, she walked down the steps as if she had just left a friend's house and turned away from the side of the house with the master bedroom.

Mack fell in step beside her, took her hand and held it like a boyfriend going out with his girl for a stroll. After a block, they turned and doubled back on the next street, hurrying toward the parked truck.

As they approached the truck, a car whipped around the corner from the direction of Pruett's house.

Riley grabbed the front of Mack's shirt and pulled him into a tight embrace, rising on her toes to slam her mouth against his.

Taking his cue, he cupped the back of her head and turned her face away from the oncoming vehicle.

What started as a kiss to hide Riley's face became something entirely different.

The car passed and turned the corner, disappearing around the houses on the next street. But Mack continued to kiss Riley, and Riley kissed him back.

She liked the way his lips were soft, but firm. Liked how hard his body was against her softer curves. Loved how he made her feel more feminine than any other man. She was familiar with every way to take a person down but was almost certain she'd struggle to overpower this man. And she liked that, too.

With one hand at the small of her back and the other buried in her hair, Mack brought her ever closer until there was no space between them. When he skimmed his tongue across the seam of her mouth, she opened eagerly, wanting to taste him, to caress him in that intimate way.

They might have gone on for a lot longer, but a car slowed in passing and a teen yelled, "Get a room!"

Riley backed away, her cheeks heating and her mouth throbbing from Mack's kiss. "Was that Pruett?" she asked, her voice shaking. Her entire body trembled with her reaction to being so close to the marine.

"I don't know. I think so."

"We should try to catch up." She stared up at him, her legs refusing to move.

Mack nodded. "We should. But I think he's too far ahead."

"Right." Riley took a deep, steadying breath and climbed into the truck.

Mack got in beside her. "Tracy's place?"

"Yeah." She fumbled with her cell phone and keyed in the address.

They drove to her house in silence, neither looking across at the other. At least not blatantly. Riley watched Mack in her peripheral vision. He didn't turn to face her once.

It took all of the thirty-minute ride for her heart to return to a regular pace and for her to talk herself down from the raging desire she'd felt in that one kiss. She wanted so much more.

By the time they reached Tracy's apartment, dusk had settled over that corner of Virginia. Tracy's apartment was completely dark from the outside.

Mack walked up to the door and knocked. If she answered, he'd make up a story or pretend he'd gotten the wrong apartment. Riley waited in the truck with the interior lights off. When no one came to the door, Riley joined Mack at the door and worked her magic with the file. They entered Tracy's apartment and moved around using a penlight Riley kept in her purse. Unlike Steve Pruett's place, Tracy's was a disaster. Clothes littered the floor, dishes were piled in the sink and the bathroom looked like it hadn't been cleaned since she moved in. Tracy wasn't there, and neither was Toby.

Riley left Tracy's place discouraged.

As they pulled out of the parking lot, a dark older-model SUV sprang out of a side street and slammed into the passenger side of Mack's pickup.

Riley was flung sideways. The seat belt tightened across her chest, keeping her rooted to her seat though her head jerked hard on her neck.

The SUV backed up, the engine revved, and the tires spun up smoke as the vehicle came at them again.

At the last moment, Mack gunned the accelerator.

The SUV hit the bed of the pickup, spinning the entire vehicle ninety degrees to the right. When the SUV backed up to hit them again, they were nose to nose.

Mack shoved the gearshift into Reverse and spun the wheel, turning the passenger side of the truck away from the SUV and taking the brunt of the attack on the front left bumper.

The SUV hit hard. The driver's side airbag deployed, shooting a bag and white dust into Mack's face. The passenger side had been turned off, giving Riley a clear view of the vehicle coming at them yet again.

"Gun it!" she yelled, and grabbed the steering wheel, jerking it to the right.

Blinking the dust out of his eyes, Mack punched his foot to the floor, sending the truck into a spin.

The SUV clipped the back end and sped away.

Mack shoved the truck into Drive, but it limped forward, grinding to a stop.

"What the hell?" Mack jumped out and stared at the front bumper.

Riley got out and stood beside him, staring down at the fender bent all the way into the front wheel. The truck wasn't going anywhere but up on a tow truck.

Whoever had hit them hadn't had a license plate on the back of his vehicle. Nor had the lights been on. All Riley could say was that it was a dark SUV. Nothing really to go on. If it was the same person who had Toby, why would he want to kill them when Charlie was still alive? Nothing made sense.

Chapter Nine

Mack called Declan. Within twenty-five minutes, his friend arrived, picked them up and took them back to Charlie's place, where her computer guy was working late, trying to find some connection among Charlie, Tracy, Pruett, Moretti and Russia. With too many angles to pursue, the search could be endless.

"Why didn't we go to my place?" Riley asked.

"Charlie didn't think it would be safe," Declan said. "She has a security system set up all around her estate. No one is getting in without her permission."

"She isn't actually calling you, is she?" Mack asked. "Cell phones can be hacked, and people could be listening in on her conversations. They'd know immediately she wasn't in that bad shape."

Declan grinned. "She passes all information through Gus and Mustang. The reports coming from her doctor to the press are that she's in critical condition, not expected to live past the next twenty-four hours."

"I'm surprised the hospital is letting her stay," Riley said. "Is her doctor even allowed to practice in that hospital?"

"Money has a way of paving the way to breaking rules," Declan said. "I think she's promised to upgrade all the medical equipment in the emergency room and all of the operating rooms and build a new children's wing."

"I wish finding Toby was that easy." Riley sat on a white sectional sofa in a large den with cathedral ceilings and windows from the floors to the twenty-foot ceilings. The house was situated on a little bit of a hill, surrounded by at least ten acres of lush landscaping. The lights of the city sparkled all around, close but not too close.

"I expected to hear from Toby's kidnapper by now." Riley scrubbed a hand through her hair. "With reports of Mrs. Halverson still showing she's hanging on, I would have thought he'd threaten me again if I didn't finish the job."

"My mother told me never to borrow trouble." Grace entered the room, her hair up in a towel, looking fresh and squeaky clean from a shower. "Hey, roommate. I'm sorry about Toby. I have some extra clothes in my suitcase if you'd like to get a shower and freshen up."

Riley sighed. "I'd like to find my brother more than anything."

"Yeah, but while you're waiting, you might as well take advantage of that incredible shower." Grace held out her hand.

Riley placed hers in her friend's and let her draw her to her feet.

Mack stood as well and waited for the women to leave the room.

"What's the scoop on Riley?" Declan asked.

Mack stiffened. "What do you mean?"

"I understand she's Russian." Declan shook his head. "You'd never know by her accent."

"Because she was raised in America, not Russia." Mack's fists clenched. "She didn't ask to be a spy."

"But she was raised for that capacity?"

"Yes. But you can't always pick your parents. What's your point?"

Declan held up his hands. "No point. I just want to make sure you're okay helping her. Charlie was pretty adamant about us helping Riley find her brother. I can't believe Riley was sent to kill Charlie."

"And she could have," Mack said. "But she didn't."

Declan's brow dipped, and his eyes narrowed. "You like the girl?"

"I didn't say that. I just know she's all about rescuing Toby. He's the only family she has left. Hell, the kid's only six."

"Gotcha." Declan draped an arm over Mack's shoulder. "We'll do everything we can to find him and bring him home."

"I get the feeling we're looking for the wrong person. Even if Pruett or the Tracy woman is involved, they had to have gotten information about Riley from her handler. That's the guy who can make or break Riley in the end. What do we know about Russian agents in the area? Can we tap into the FBI or CIA? Does Charlie have any connections on that front?"

"She does. Or her husband did, and she does because of him. Come meet Jonah Spradlin. He worked with Mr. Halverson on a special project and still works for Charlie. He's amazing with the internet and anything computer. And he's prior military."

"Marine?"

"No, but almost as good. He was in the navy."

Mack followed Declan through the maze of rooms and corridors in the sprawling mansion. He stopped at a doorway with a hand scanner affixed to a panel near the doorknob.

Declan pressed his palm to the pad. A moment later a lock clicked, and the door swung open. He briefly glanced toward Mack. "Don't worry, the entire team will be set up to enter the war room when Jonah can get around to it. Right now he's busy working this case. He's barely stopped to eat since he started."

"Good to know someone is on it. We haven't made much headway chasing people."

"Jonah assures me he can find just about anything in the data."

They descended stairs into a basement with a large table down the middle of the room, computer monitors lining one wall and a huge whiteboard across another wall.

A man sat in the far corner in front of an array of six large monitors. He bent over the keyboard, typing away, his attention on the monitor directly in front of him. Every so often, he'd glance to one of the other screens.

"Jonah, Mack's here. You two should put your heads together on finding Toby. And when Riley gets down here, she might have even more insight into who might have her brother."

The man at the keyboard held up a finger. "Hold on." He keyed some more, stared at the monitor and frowned. "I might have something here." Jonah turned to Mack. "Declan said you went by Pruett's house?"

Mack nodded. "We did, but we didn't find anything there. He came home while we were hiding in his basement, but we made it out before he caught us."

Jonah held out his hand. "Which house did you go to?"

Mack frowned as he shook the computer guy's hand. "What do you mean?"

"Real estate records show that he owns more than one." Jonah released Mack's hand and turned back to the monitor. He clicked a couple keys and brought up images of two houses.

Mack leaned over his shoulder and pointed to one. "We went to that one."

Jonah pointed to the other. "He has this one on a lake in the next county. The bank has threatened to foreclose on it."

"I don't get it. The guy's other house doesn't appear too extravagant. What's he spending his money on?"

"I looked into his bank records. He likes expensive cars and vacations. He's been to Bora-Bora more than once in the past two years and to a high-end all-inclusive resort in the Caymans a number of times. And he doesn't go alone."

"Who is he taking?"

"I'm working on that. I couldn't get that information from his bank records, but I'm tapping into the resort databases, hoping to get passport data from the rooms he secured."

"Anything I can do to help?" Mack asked.

"You can go through his phone records and see

if you find anything else. If you find a number he's used in the past couple days more than once, you can enter it here." Jonah pointed to another monitor. "It'll bring up who it belongs to, unless it's a blocked number. In that case, I'll have to do a little more digging. Is there anyone else we should be looking at?"

"What about the nanny?" Declan asked.

"I've met Margaret Weems. She's an older woman who seemed pretty upset that Toby was taken."

"In a lot of abduction cases, the child is taken by someone close to the family, if not a family member," Jonah pointed out. He made a note on a piece of paper. "Margaret Weems?"

"That's her name," Mack confirmed.

"I'll check on her," Jonah said. "In the meantime, you can get started on Pruett's phone records."

"I'm on it." Mack pulled up a rolling chair, sat at a computer keyboard beside Jonah and immersed himself in sifting through data.

"I'll see about getting some food brought down to you," Declan said.

Mack didn't hear him leave. He was so focused on the numbers and looking up who they belonged to that he tuned out all else.

Until Riley entered the room and stood behind him, resting her hand on his shoulder. As he brought up the numbers, she commented when she recognized one.

"That's Paul Robles, our project leader's number,"

she said. "The man has three kids of his own and two adopted from fostering. He doesn't have time to kidnap another."

Soon she pulled up a chair beside him and leaned over his arm to read the names on the screen.

Declan delivered sandwiches, which they ate while poring over the phone records of Pruett, Young and Tracy Gibson. Nothing appeared out of the ordinary for a team of aerospace professionals communicating on a group project.

After midnight, Riley laid her head on the desk, blinking hard to keep from falling asleep.

Mack fought fatigue until he finally gave up and rose from his chair. "Come on, let's find a place to sleep."

Riley yawned but didn't lift her head from the desk. "I'm good right here."

"You two get some rest." Declan said. "I'm betting you've been going since last night."

"Up for over thirty-six hours," Mack confirmed.

When Riley didn't rise, he bent and scooped her up in his arms.

"Hey, I can walk on my own," she said, though her head lolled back, and she closed her eyes, snuggling into his chest. "But this is easier."

Mack strode across the room and climbed the stairs.

Riley roused enough to open the door but closed her eyes again when Mack stepped through.

Declan met them in the living room. "There's a room for each of you down the hall. Doesn't matter which you take. First two doors on the right. I think Grace left some clothes for Riley in the first one. And one other thing." Declan held out his hand. "Keep this on you, Riley. In case whoever set you up for this assignment decides to take you." He placed a small metal disk in her hand.

"What is it?" she asked.

"A GPS tracking device," Declan said. "We can follow where you go, should you get separated from Mack."

She frowned. "Are you afraid I'll run off?"

Declan smiled. "Not at all. It's more for your safety in case we can't get to you soon enough."

Riley slipped the disk into her pocket and leaned her head against Mack's chest. "Thank you for your concern over my welfare. It's more than I deserve."

"Thanks, Declan," Mack called over his shoulder as he turned and headed for the first door.

The spacious room had been prepared by one of Charlie's staff, the comforter turned back and the pillows fluffed. A powder-blue nightgown lay spread out on the white comforter.

"This one's yours." Mack lowered her legs, letting her body slide down his until her feet hit the floor. "I'll be next door if you need me."

She touched his arm. "Thank you for helping me."

"I haven't done anything yet."

"Yes, you have." Riley tilted her head to the right and then left. "If I'd been on my own in my car, that SUV would have wiped me out." She tipped her head to the right again and winced.

"Are you pretty sore from the attack?"

She shrugged and grimaced. "I guess I am a little more than I thought."

Mack turned her around and rested his warm hands on her skin where her neck met her shoulders.

"Um, that feels good." She leaned her head forward and relaxed.

Mack gently rubbed the back of her neck and shoulders, carefully kneading the knots out of her muscles.

The more he touched her, the more he wanted to touch. His groin tightened, and he shifted to relieve the pressure.

"I'd better go," he said, and dropped his hands to his sides, afraid if he lingered any longer he'd want to stay the night.

Riley turned and wrapped her arms around his waist. "Thank you for all you're doing to find Toby." She pressed her cheek to his chest. "I don't know where I'd have begun without your help."

"Thank me when we get him back." He gripped her arms and set her to arm's length. "Now, I'd better go to my own room before I do something I'll regret."

Riley looked up at him with her big sleepy hazel eyes. "Like what?"

"Like kiss you," he said. And he did. He leaned forward with the intention of only brushing his lips across hers, ever so softly. But as soon as his mouth connected with hers, he knew he couldn't stop.

When Riley's arms circled his neck and brought him closer, he was a goner.

He clamped his arms around her waist and pulled her body against his. The hardness of his erection pressing into the softness of her belly. He groaned, knowing this wasn't the time or place.

His tongue darted out and met no resistance.

She parted her lips and accepted him in, curling her own tongue around his in a long, sensual caress.

Mack weaved his hands into her hair, loving how soft and thick it was against his skin. She was beautiful, strong and yet vulnerable.

When he brought his head up, he drew in a deep steadying breath. "I should go."

"Stay," she said on a breath of warm air that feathered across his chin and neck.

Mack moaned and fought his desire, knowing he couldn't take advantage of her when she was so worried about her brother. "I can't."

"Can't or won't?" she said. "I won't ask anything of you. Just stay with me. Please."

"If I stay, I won't be able to keep my hands off you."

Her eyes widened. "So?"

"So, I can't stay and not touch you." He shook his head.

"Then touch me," she said. "Because I want to touch you, too." As if to prove her point, she slipped her hands beneath his T-shirt and splayed her fingers across his chest. "Stay with me. I don't want to be alone tonight."

Mack was tempted. But the woman was an admitted Russia sleeper agent. If he slept with her, his loyalty to his country could be in question.

Ah, who was he kidding? He'd been dishonorably discharged from the military. His loyalty was already in question by others. But not to himself. He was still the same marine who'd give his life for his country and the citizens he'd sworn to protect and serve.

In his heart, he knew this woman wasn't one of the bad guys. She was a victim of her birth, of her upbringing. But she loved her little brother and would do anything to get him back.

And, like Riley, Mack would have done anything to save his brother, had he been given a chance.

They weren't all that different from each other. And she felt right in his arms.

Riley leaned up on her toes and pressed her lips

to his. "If you don't want to stay, I understand." She cupped the back of his head and brought his mouth to hers in a long, warm and wet kiss.

It was his undoing. Mack scooped her legs out from under her and laid her on the bed. He climbed up to lie on the comforter beside her, deepening the kiss she'd started. What began as two mouths meeting soon turned into his hands exploring the curved surfaces of her body.

Riley sat up, pulled her shirt over her head and tossed it to the side. Then she reached for Mack's T-shirt, dragging it up over his head.

He raised his arms and took it the rest of the way, slinging it to a far corner. He lay beside Riley, trailing a finger over the curve of her breast, the indentation of her waist and the swell of her hip. "You're beautiful."

She traced a line from his collarbone, across his chest and down to one of the hard brown nipples, where she pinched it between her fingers and rolled it into a tight little bead. "You're not so hard to look at, you know."

"We don't have to do anything but hold each other," he said. "I'd be happy with that."

"You would?" she asked, looking up with a furrowed brow. "Because I wouldn't be nearly as satisfied." Her fingers trailed down his torso to his belly button and lower to the waistband of his jeans.

"Be with me tonight. In every sense of the word," she whispered.

Mack gave up the good fight to remain unfazed by her touch and embraced all of what she offered. He gathered her close, pressed his lips to her temple and then her cheek. He trailed a path from her lips, across her chin and down the long, smooth line of her neck to the pulse beating wildly at the base.

Riley moaned and writhed beneath him, her back arching, brushing the lace of her bra across his naked chest. The coarse texture sent a thrill of excitement straight south, making him grow and harden.

Mack shifted on the bed, rising to lean over Riley. "Say the word and I stop here."

She shook her head and reached for the button on his jeans. "Don't stop. I want what you have. I need you to be with me. I need life to continue on." Riley flicked the button through the hole and lowered his zipper.

He sprang free into her palm and nearly lost himself there. But he held back, determined to give her just as much pleasure as he was already feeling.

All his fatigue disappeared in a rush of adrenaline. He rolled off the bed, shucked his jeans. Then he leaned over Riley, unbuttoned her jeans and slid them down her legs. Once she was free of them, he trailed his fingers up the inside of her calf, knee and thigh to her hot center. Her panties were damp from her juices, making Mack want to tear them off with his teeth. Instead he hooked his thumb in the elastic and tugged them over her hips and thighs in a long, slow glide, following the path of her panties with his tongue.

Once the silk underwear cleared her ankles, she let her knees fall to the sides.

Mack worked his way back up her long, smooth legs, brushing his lips across every inch of her skin. He didn't stop until he reached her entrance.

"Protection?" she gasped, her breath hitching in her throat.

"Got it." Mack bent to where he'd shed his jeans, pulled his wallet from the back pocket and unearthed a packet. He held it out to her.

She took it, tore it open and rolled it down over his staff. "I want you, Mack. Now."

He smiled. "I want you, too. But first you."

RILEY WAS ALREADY so close to losing herself, she moaned her frustration.

When Mack slipped a finger inside her channel and swirled it around, Riley nearly came undone. Then he dragged it up to that bundle of tightly packed nerves at her center.

Riley dug her heels into the mattress and raised her hips to meet his assault on her senses. Every muscle in her body tensed, and tingling began at her center, spreading outward. She couldn't breathe and couldn't think beyond what he was doing to her. For a brief moment in time, she forgot about her worries, about Toby, about everything as she shot over the edge and rocketed into the stratosphere.

For what felt like forever and yet only a moment, she spiraled out of control.

When she drifted back to earth, she gripped Mack's shoulders and dragged him up her body.

He settled between her legs and touched his shaft to her entrance.

Beyond any kind of patience, she clutched his buttocks and pulled him into her.

He was hot and thick, filling her and stretching her in a long, delicious glide.

Riley rose to meet him thrust for thrust until they rocked the bed in rhythm.

He tensed, his body going as rigid as his shaft. Thrusting one last time, he buried himself inside her.

Riley held him there, her fingers digging into his buttocks. She'd never felt anything quite as satisfying as making love with Mack and suspected she'd never feel this way with any other man.

He collapsed against her and rolled them both to their sides without losing their intimate connection.

Riley snuggled close, pressing her cheek to his chest, inhaling the musky, male scent of the man.

Exhaustion pulled at her eyelids, and she gave in to sleep.

As she drifted off, his voice rumbled against her. "We'll find him. I promise."

Chapter Ten

Mack lay awake after Riley fell asleep, wondering how he would keep his promise to find her brother. He wanted to keep that promise more than anything. But they had so little to go on.

After a while, he gave up on sleep and returned to the door leading to the computer room.

"Couldn't sleep?" Declan padded barefoot in from the direction of the kitchen, carrying a steaming mug. "I made a pot of coffee."

"I could use some. Point me in the direction of the kitchen?"

"I can do better than that. This place is huge and can be confusing." He tipped his head. "Come on."

Mack followed Declan into a huge gourmet kitchen. Jonah sat at a massive table, eating a massive sandwich stuffed full of deli meat.

Jonah chewed what was in his mouth and swallowed before saying, "Not finding much on those names you gave me. Still looking for the exact location of Pruett's lake house. It shows up in court records as lots and plats. It's on a rural route, which to me says dirt road. When I have it, I'll get that address to you ASAP."

"Good. I've been thinking about it. You might also expand your search to anyone with access to Riley's office after hours at Quest. Only someone who came in after hours would have been able to set the camera in the light fixture."

"Will get right on it after I finish my breakfast, lunch and dinner." Jonah held up the sandwich.

Mack chuckled. "Fair enough. You have to fuel the body, even if you don't need sleep."

"You got that right." Jonah bit into his sandwich with a healthy growl.

"How's Riley holding up?" Declan asked.

"She's exhausted. I imagine the worry is eating away at her."

"I can't get over that she's a trained Russian spy."

Mack stiffened. "Riley's a product of her parents. She didn't sign up for it or want it."

"Still, there had to be some brainwashing along the way. The Russians are really good at raising their own secret agents. Are we sure we can trust her?"

Mack remembered how he felt inside her and the

way she gave herself to him completely. "Can you trust every American you meet?"

Declan shrugged. "Not everyone. We have our own homegrown terrorists and zealots who've got a beef against our government. They'd just as soon shoot you as give you the time of day."

"Yeah, but a trained sleeper spy…" Jonah shook his head. "It's a lot to ask to trust someone who was sent to this country for the benefit of Russia. Their leader isn't above using every asset at his disposal to take what he wants."

"Yeah, he's a wild card," Mack agreed.

"As concerned as she is about her brother, I doubt she's a threat to us."

"Maybe not now. But what about when she finds Toby?" Declan asked. "She needs us now. She's not going to kill those who can help her, until they are of no more assistance to her."

Mack's instincts had been pretty spot-on for most of his career in the military. His gut told him Riley was one of the good guys. "Charlie trusts her."

Declan turned to face Mack, his eyebrows raised. "Yeah, but do you trust her?"

"I—" A noise drew Mack's attention away from the conversation. But when he turned toward the living area, no one was there. He might have imagined it, or the sound echoed off the wall close to where Declan was making another pot of coffee. He shook his head and tried to remember the question. "The fact that she didn't kill our boss says a lot. She could have done exactly what her handler wanted and gotten her brother back sooner."

"Or not."

"Either way, she didn't kill Charlie. In fact, I pulled her off Charlie."

Declan's eyes narrowed. "She physically attacked Charlie?"

"Charlie had the poison Riley was supposed to give her. She threatened to take it herself so that Riley wouldn't lose her brother. Riley fought Charlie for that poison. She wouldn't let her take it."

"Are you sure that was what she was doing?"

Mack nodded. "Positive. And Charlie would back it up. Riley went to the gala with the intention of doing whatever it took to get her brother back. But when the rubber hit the road, she couldn't do it. She might be trained as a Russian spy, with all the skills necessary to survive in that role, but she doesn't have the heart to kill an innocent woman."

Declan handed Mack a cup of coffee. "Sounds like you've made up your mind about the woman."

"I have."

"And it doesn't have anything to do with her being a knockout?"

"No. She's the real deal. I'd trust her with my life."

"I hope you're right." Declan frowned. "Because

you might be playing with fire if you put your faith in her."

Mack's back stiffened. "I'll take my chances with Riley. I know I'm right about her."

Declan's frown cleared. "Can I get you something to eat?"

"No. The coffee is all I need for now. I need to get back to work. I'm not good with sitting around waiting for something to happen."

"None of us are," Declan said. "But we don't have a lot we can do until we know what we're up against. What's your next move?"

"We need to find Steve Pruett's lake house and pay it a visit." He hoped like hell they found Toby there. Time was running out for Riley and the kid.

RILEY HAD WOKEN to an empty bed. A glance at the clock indicated it was just past midnight. She pulled the sheet up over her naked breasts and stared around the room, lit only by the starlight shining through the window. Where had Mack gone? Did he regret making love to her?

She didn't regret it at all, though it complicated their working relationship and could only make it more awkward. Still, she couldn't regret having had the best sex she'd ever experienced. The man's lips were magic.

Her body heated with the memory, and she was

deliciously sore. Riley moaned softly and ran her hand over her breasts and down the tuft of hair over her sex. She'd really made love to a man she'd only known a short time. What had she been thinking?

That she needed to hold someone and be held. When the odds were stacked against her, she had Mack to lean on, to help her find her way through the maze of clues. If anyone could help her find her brother, Mack was the one to do it.

She tossed the sheet aside, pulled on her clothes and tiptoed, barefoot, across the floor to the door. When she opened it, she hoped to find Mack on the other side, on his way back to bed with her.

He wasn't there. Curious now, she wandered down the hallway. Voices sounded from across the wide expanse of living area to another room Riley supposed was the kitchen.

Barefoot, her feet made no sound on the wooden floors. Not until she reached the entryway into the kitchen did she realize the men in the kitchen were talking about her.

More than once, Mack's friend Declan said the word *Russian*.

Riley eased up to the doorway and cocked her head to better hear what they were saying.

When Declan asked Mack if he trusted her, Riley froze in place. Mack hesitated with his answer.

Her heart leaped into her throat, threatening to cut off the air to her brain. Mack didn't trust her.

Her pulse pumped so hard against her eardrums she couldn't hear his response. Her chest hurt so bad she could barely draw a breath. Riley spun and ran from the living room back to the bedroom, where she grabbed her cell phone, called a car service and gave him the address of Charlie's estate.

Then she pulled on her shoes, hooked her purse over her arm and slipped out a French door onto a patio. Making her way around the house, she paralleled the driveway, clinging to the shadows as she hurried toward the exit. At the gate, she made note of the camera. So what if Mack saw her leaving? He didn't trust her anyway. He'd think the worst, that she was skipping out, maybe to complete the job of killing Charlie.

Well, he could think what he wanted. He probably only stuck to her like glue to keep an eye on her.

Why, oh why, had she slept with the man?

She stood still, staring at the gate without really seeing it. She'd slept with him because she'd felt a connection so deep she'd thought it was real. It had been…on her part. But apparently not on his.

Riley looked the gate over for a button to open the heavy iron bars but couldn't find one. Headlights turned onto the street and slowed as they approached.

Not wanting to buzz the house to let her out, she

climbed up a tree beside the stone wall, looped her leg over the top and dropped to the other side.

The car slid to a stop.

For a moment, Riley thought it might be the person who'd tried to bash the hell out of Mack's truck. Bunching her muscles, she prepared to make a break for it.

The car stopped beside her and the passenger window slid down. "You the lady who called for a ride?"

"Yes," she said.

"Good. I wasn't sure about the address. Never been in this neighborhood." He stared up at the lights shining down on the massive stone gate. "Fancy place."

"Yes, it is."

Riley yanked open the back door and slid into the back seat.

Even before she had her seat belt completely fastened, the driver pulled away from the gate, heading toward her apartment.

She'd get her car and continue her search on her own. She didn't need the liability of someone who couldn't believe in her. In her heart, she knew she was one of the good guys. She couldn't kill an innocent person. She could kill, if she had to defend someone she loved, but not at the command of another just because that person had a grudge. If Mack couldn't see past Riley's upbringing to the person beneath her skin, he was missing who she really was.

In her mind, she circled back to the most important issue at hand. Finding Toby.

Steve Pruett had a lake house. All she had to do was find that house and find Toby. She didn't need a former marine to hold her hand through the process. She was a trained assassin and spy. She could handle anything anyone could throw her way.

MACK LEFT THE kitchen and returned to the bedroom where he'd left Riley sleeping. As soon as he walked through the door, he knew something was wrong. The bed was a jumble, the sheets half on the floor, the comforter pushed to the end of the empty bed. A quick glance around the room confirmed his fear.

Riley's clothes were gone, along with her purse. He checked in the adjoining bathroom but knew before he did that she wouldn't be there.

He ran back down the hallway to the kitchen.

Declan and Jonah glanced up.

"Riley's gone," he said.

Declan pushed himself away from the counter and set his mug down. "Are you sure?"

A lead weight sank to the pit of Mack's gut. "Positive."

"Hang on, I'll tell you where she is." Jonah touched

the screen on his phone and brought up the security monitors. "She's jumping the front gate as we speak."

"Damn." Mack slammed his fist into his palm.

Declan glanced at the video. "Where do you think she's going?"

"I don't know," Mack said. "She doesn't have Pruett's second address." He paced the kitchen floor. "She could be going back to her apartment." He glanced up. "I'll go there and see if I can catch up to her. I hope she's all right. After the SUV attacked my truck, I don't think she's safe out there on her own."

"We'll get that address to you as soon as we find it," Declan said. "Did you give Riley the tracking disk?"

Mack nodded. "I did."

"Good." Declan's lips pressed together in a tight line. "It makes it easier for us to track her."

Mack's lips tilted upward. "She was happy we cared enough to give her one."

"Does she understand it's not for us to spy on her, but to keep her safe in case she ends up in the wrong hands?"

Again, Mack nodded. "Yes."

"Good." Declan tipped his chin. "You'd better get going. And take this truck." He handed Mack a set of keys.

"Thanks." Then he ran out the door and down the steps. He was in his replacement truck backing away from the house when a call came through his phone. He hit the talk button on his steering wheel. "Yeah."

"Mack, Jonah here. I went further back on Pruett's phone records and got a hit on one of the phone numbers. He placed several calls to a Tracy Gibson last month after hours. The calls ended about the time Moretti was killed and Tracy was laid off."

"Good to know. Thanks."

"Also, texting the address of Pruett's lake cabin. It's out there and on a dirt road. Not many houses show up in that area. If he's hiding the boy there, no one would know."

"I'll get right on it as soon as I find Riley."

"Gotcha," Jonah said. "In the meantime, I can get other members of the team to lead the investigation of Pruett's lake house."

"No. I'll get Riley and head that way. She'll want to go in. The boy will want to see someone he knows. Have the team gather and wait on standby. If anything goes south, I'll need assistance ASAP."

"We've got your back," Jonah said. "Just say the word and we'll be there. Well, Declan will be there for you. I'd come, but I think I'd be better at manning the computers, trackers and other technical support. But if you need me there, I'll come."

"No worries. Sometimes it's easier to get in and out with fewer people."

"Okay," Jonah said. "I'll keep you up to date."

"Don't forget to send me Pruett's lake cabin address."

"On it," Jonah said. "Out here."

Mack sped to Riley's apartment, barely slowing for the light signals. He couldn't get there fast enough. All the while, he wondered what had spooked her and why she'd felt the need to go after her brother on her own. Had making love to her scared her so badly she wanted to get away from him? If that was the case, he'd keep his hands to himself until they found Toby. After he'd made love to Riley, not touching her would be difficult. He wanted to hold her in his arms and take all her pain and worry away. And he wanted to make love to her again and again. The woman was sensual, sexy and amazing in bed.

Why the hell had she run?

Chapter Eleven

The drive to Riley's apartment passed in a blur. When she arrived, she dug in her purse for the key and let herself in. Focused on what she had to do next, she hurried across the threshold of the front door. A sound behind her made her pause. Footsteps?

She started to turn but was shoved from behind so hard she stumbled into the apartment, lost her balance and fell hard to her knees. She hadn't expected to be attacked, but she should have reacted faster. Her father would have been disappointed in her response.

The door slammed behind her and a sharp-toed shoe slammed into Riley's ribs.

She grunted and rolled to her side, looking up at the woman who'd just kicked the crap out of her. She knew the woman, but not in the context of her apartment.

"Tracy?" Riley clutched at her throbbing rib. "What the hell?"

"You're the one who started all this mess. You're the one who got Mr. Moretti killed and me fired. If you hadn't meddled, I'd still be working at Quest, and Steve wouldn't have dumped me."

Tracy cocked her leg and shot out another kick.

This time Riley was ready for it. Twisting to the right, she avoided the sharp-toed shoe, snagged the woman's ankle and pulled hard.

Tracy screeched and threw her hands in the air, searching for purchase, finding none. She crashed to the floor, landing hard on her back. She lay for a moment, stunned.

Riley rolled over and straddled the woman, pinning her wrists to either side of her head. "First of all, Moretti got himself killed by dealing with the wrong people. He was selling proprietary secrets to a foreign country. I didn't make him do that. I just helped the FBI to discover who was dealing dirty."

"So he sold some secrets. They'd have gotten them anyway. Computers can be hacked. Nothing is secret anymore." Tracy bucked beneath Riley, but she couldn't go anywhere.

"As for getting you fired, that was HR," Riley reminded her. "With Moretti gone, they had no use for a secretary to an empty position."

"I needed that job. I have a mortgage and bills to

pay. Do you know how hard it is to find a job that pays as well?" Tracy jerked at her arms. "Let go of me. This is all your fault."

"And what do you mean by Steve dumped you? Steve Pruett? I didn't even know he dated."

"He did," Tracy practically spat out. "Me! Until a few days ago. Then he called and said he was done. Dropped my clothes and toothbrush off on my front porch and hasn't returned my calls since." Tears welled in her eyes. "He's done. And it's all your fault." She bucked again. "I hate you, Riley Lansing. You're poison!"

Riley couldn't help feeling sorry for the woman. But her hardship wasn't Riley's fault so much as Tracy's bad luck with her boss and poor choice of a boyfriend.

"Do you know where Steve's lake house is?" Riley asked.

She snorted. "Yes, of course. We spent weekends there before he dumped me. But what's it to you?"

"Tell me where his cabin is, and I'll see if I can get you back on at Quest."

"Why should I tell you where Steve's lake cabin is? Isn't it enough he dumped me? Now you're making a play for the man?" Trace shook her head. "No way."

"Fine, I'll just call the police and report you for

assault. If you have a criminal record, you'll never find a job."

The woman sagged beneath her and stopped struggling. "Oh, what's the use anyway? I've lost Steve. I don't have a job, and I'm going to lose my house. If I go to jail, at least I'll have a roof over my head and three meals a day." Tears leaked from her eyes. "Go ahead, call the police."

Frustrated beyond patience, Riley bit back a curse. "I'd rather you tell me where Steve's lake cabin is."

"Why do you want to know?"

"He has something of mine that I want back."

"Find him yourself," Tracy said. "I owe you nothing."

For a long moment, Riley stared down at the woman with tears dripping down the sides of her face. "I'm sorry this all happened to you, but it's important that I find Steve. Please, tell me where I can find his cabin."

Tracy sighed. "Let me up, and I'll tell you."

Riley frowned. "You're not going to try anything, are you?"

"What could I try? You're clearly better at fighting and pinning someone than I am." Tracy didn't pull at her wrists or move beneath Riley.

Shifting slowly, Riley released Tracy's wrists, one by one. Then she swung her leg off the woman and pushed herself to her feet.

Tracy lay for a moment on her back.

Riley reached out a hand to her.

The woman grabbed her hand and let her pull her to her feet. "I'll tell you where Steve's cabin is if you don't turn me over to the police." Tracy gave her an address.

Riley repeated it to her, committing it to memory. Then she opened the door and held it for Tracy. "You should go now. And just so you know, I'm sorry you lost your job."

Tracy bent to retrieve a small backpack from the floor by the door and turned in the doorframe. "Moretti was an idiot. He had a good thing going at Quest. He shouldn't have gotten involved in selling secrets."

"No, he shouldn't have," Riley agreed.

"And I shouldn't have turned a blind eye to his activities." She dug in the backpack as if unearthing keys. "But you know—" Tracy pulled a small handgun out and aimed it at Riley "—you shouldn't have set him up."

Riley stared at the gun, her pulse quickening, her thoughts racing through several scenarios. "Do you even know how to use that thing?"

Tracy stared down at the gun in her hand. "There's not much to it. You point and shoot." She raised her arm, leveling the weapon at Riley's chest. "If I'm going to jail, it might as well be for a damned good reason."

Riley could see when the woman's finger tightened on the trigger. She dived to the side in a flying somersault and rolled to her feet.

The gun went off, hitting the wall behind where Riley had been standing the moment before.

Tracy swung the gun toward Riley's new location. Before she could pull the trigger again, a man stepped up behind her and grabbed her around the waist, clamping her arms downward against her sides.

The gun went off, the bullet hitting the floor beside Tracy's foot. "Let go of me!" she screamed.

"Not until you drop the gun," Mack's deep, resonant voice said.

Riley's heart swelled in her chest as she rose to face Tracy and Mack. She grabbed the gun from Tracy's hand, dropped the magazine from the handle and expelled the round in the chamber. When she was done, she stared over Tracy's shoulder at Mack. "Thanks."

Mack gave Riley a slight chin lift. "Call the police."

Riley shook her head. "We don't have time. She gave me the address to Steve's lake cabin. I'm going now." Riley swiped her car keys off the table in the hallway and stepped past Mack holding Tracy.

Mack's hand shot out and he grabbed Riley's arm. He repositioned his other arm to clamp Tracy in his grip. "You're not going on your own."

"I don't need anyone's help." She lifted her chin, her lips pressing together. "This is my problem. I'll take care of it."

"You can't go there alone. If Steve's desperate, he could do anything."

She squared her shoulders. "I'm willing to take that risk."

"Even if it means Toby will be hurt?" Mack pinned her with his gaze.

For a long moment, Riley stared into his blue eyes, and then her shoulders sagged, just a little. "No."

Mack glanced down at the woman in his grip. "We can't leave her. She might give Steve a heads-up."

Riley twisted her lips. "I'm not staying to babysit her. If there's a chance we can find Toby, I want to be there. The kid has to be beside himself and scared."

"My phone is in my back pocket." Mack tilted his head to the side. "Get it. Call Declan. Tell him what's going on and ask him to send a backup to hold this woman until we can get to Pruett's lake cabin."

"He won't be there," Tracy said.

"Why do you say that?" Riley asked.

"It's being renovated," she said. "He hasn't been visiting the cabin for the past few weeks."

"Would he go anywhere else?"

Tracy shrugged. "Where else would he go? His parents live in Ohio, and he doesn't have any close friends or siblings in the area."

Riley met Mack's gaze. "We have to check. It's the only other place I can think of."

Mack nodded. "We will."

Tracy's eyes narrowed. "What's Steve got that you want? Is he stealing secrets like Mr. Moretti? If so, he can rot in hell with Moretti."

"I don't know if he was stealing secrets, but he took something I care a great deal about." Riley hesitated telling Tracy that Pruett might have taken her little brother. Not many people knew she had a brother. And from the way Tracy was acting, she didn't know what Steve was up to. If Steve had dumped her several days before, he might not have wanted her to know about the kidnapping he would undertake. If, in fact, he was the kidnapper who'd taken Toby.

Tracy squirmed in Mack's grasp. "You can't hold me forever."

"Oh, we won't," Mack said. "As soon as help arrives, we'll be gone."

Riley placed the call to Declan. While she waited, Riley keyed the address into her cell phone and brought up the directions to get to Pruett's lake cabin. Thirty minutes away. She tapped her foot, counting the seconds until help arrived, freeing her and Mack to go after Pruett.

Within ten excruciating minutes, Declan arrived at her apartment with Mustang.

"We'll take her from here." Declan and Mustang each took an arm and led Tracy into Riley's apartment. "Let us know what you find."

"Will do," Mack called out.

Riley was already through the door. She ran toward her car and slipped in behind the steering wheel.

Mack quickly caught up and dropped into the passenger seat, folding his long legs into the car.

She didn't wait for him to close the door before she pulled out of the parking lot and onto the street. Then she pressed her foot to the accelerator, racing down the dark street toward the edge of the city and out into the countryside.

For the first five minutes, silence reigned inside the confines of the vehicle.

Riley was fine with that. She didn't have much to say to Mack.

"Why did you leave Charlie's place without letting us know?"

Riley stiffened, but she forced a shrug. "I needed to move on and find my brother. Why does it matter?"

"I thought we were doing this together. What made you change your mind?"

"It doesn't matter."

"To me, it does." He turned in his seat and faced her.

Riley kept her attention on the road, but she could see him clearly in her peripheral vision and the light from the dash. His brow furrowed, and his lips were drawn into a line.

"Why?"

"Maybe I read you wrong, but I thought we had something special going."

Her chest tightened. "Or not. What's special without trust?"

His frown deepened. "What are you talking about?"

"A partnership can only work if the two people trust each other."

"What have I done to lose your trust?" he asked.

"My trusting you isn't the issue."

"I don't know what you're talking about."

"It doesn't matter."

"Yes. It. Does." He touched her arm lightly.

Even as lightly as he touched her, it made her flinch and swerve.

Mack pulled back his arm and sat back in his seat, his lips pressed together. "We can talk about this after we get to the cabin."

A heavy weight settled in Riley's belly. "Or

maybe we don't need to talk about anything. We really don't have anything to talk about, anyway."

Mack tilted his head, frowning. "Have I done something to make you mad?"

Riley focused on the road ahead. "No."

"Yeah, I can see that." He sighed. "You can tell me what's wrong, or I can continue asking questions until I hit on the right issue. Either way, I'm a patient man."

When she didn't answer, he nodded. "Okay. Was it something to do with the way we made love?"

She shot a quick glance his way. "No, of course not."

He nodded. "Good to know. Was it something I said?"

Riley's jaw tightened. "I'm not playing games with you, Mack."

"So it was something I said." He touched a finger to his chin. "I can't remember specifically what I said, but I'm sure I put my foot in my mouth on more than one occasion."

"Oh, for Pete's sake," Riley exclaimed. "Partners are supposed to trust each other."

"Yes…and?"

"And you don't trust me." There, she'd said it. "And why should you? I'm Russian. As far as anyone is concerned, I should be deported, sent back to my mother country, banned from ever returning to the United States." Her chest squeezed so hard she could barely breathe. "Only I don't know Russia. I grew up here. I can barely speak the language." She hit the steering wheel with the palm of her hand. "Damn it, I love this country. It's my home. I'd do anything to protect her."

"Pull into the gas station at the next exit." Mack pointed to the exit sign indicating a gas station.

"No." Riley sniffed, a tear finding its way down her cheek. "We have to get to the lake cabin before something horrible happens to my brother. Trust me or not, I'm going to find my brother. And if we have to leave the country, we'll leave together. As a family."

"Riley, pull over." This time he spoke in a much more commanding tone.

She gripped the steering wheel harder as they approached the exit, refusing to slow her trajectory. "I won't let them hurt my brother."

"We won't get to your brother if you don't pull off and put fuel in the tank," he pointed out. "Pull off."

A quick glance at the gas gauge brought Riley out of her pity party. She yanked the steering wheel at the last moment and sent the car onto the exit ramp and into the service station. When she rolled to a stop at a pump, she sat for a moment, her entire body shaking. A chuckle started low in her belly and rose up her throat in hysterical laughter, which quickly turned to a sob. "See? I make a lousy spy."

Mack got out of the vehicle, came around the side, jammed his credit card into the machine, activated the pump and stuck it into the tank. Then he yanked open her door and held out his hand.

Riley looked up at him through a wash of tears. "You don't trust me."

He didn't wait for her to put her hand in his; instead, he pried her fingers off the steering wheel, dragged her out of the vehicle and into his arms. "You are one stubborn, hardheaded woman, you know that?"

She remained stiff in his embrace, her hands resting on his chest, though she didn't push him away. "Why are you helping me?"

"Because Charlie asked me to and—"

"And she trusts me." Riley laughed, without humor. "Though why she would trust me, I don't know. I tried to kill her."

"No on both counts." With one hand around her, Mack reached out with the other and tucked a strand of her hair back behind her ear. "I was helping you, at first, because Charlie asked me to. Now, because I care. And quit putting words into my mouth. I don't know where you get the idea that I don't trust you."

She didn't want to admit she'd eavesdropped on

his conversation. Riley looked over his shoulder. "I can tell."

"Then you don't know me." He pressed a kiss to her forehead. "I wouldn't make love with a woman I don't trust." He brushed his lips across the tip of her nose.

Riley lifted her chin, a shiver of awareness rippling through her veins. "Lots of spies make love to people they don't trust to get information out of them."

"Is that why you made love with me?" He pulled back, a frown pulling at his brow.

She shifted her gaze to his, unable to look away. "No," Riley whispered.

Mack gripped her shoulders. "Why did you make love with me?"

Her lips trembled, and she hated herself for showing her vulnerability. "Why does it matter?"

"Because you matter to me. A lot." He let go of her shoulders and cupped her cheeks between his palms. "For some crazy reason, I like you. I want to get to know you better. And I'd want to help you even if Charlie wasn't in the picture."

She frowned up at him, her heart swelling. "You would?"

"Yes." His lips tipped upward. "And I trust you."

"Even though I'm a Russian spy?"

A smile spread across his face. "Maybe even more so because you're a lousy Russian spy."

Her frown deepened. "I'm not lousy. I just didn't want to kill Charlie after all she'd done for me."

"My point exactly." He pulled her close and pressed his lips to hers in a brief, hard kiss. "I trust you, and I want to make love to you again. But most of all, I like you and want to get to know you better."

The pump clicked off, signaling the end of their brief break.

"We need to get moving," Mack said, almost as if he regretted having to let go of her.

Riley nodded.

"Want me to drive from here?" he asked.

Yeah, she might be giving up control, and that might appear weak, but her hands shook and she couldn't seem to catch her breath when Mack held her so closely. "Yes, please."

He walked her around to the other side of the car, held the door for her and helped her into her seat. Then he hurried to replace the pump handle and screw the gas cap on. A few moments later, they were on the road again.

Riley stared at the pavement in front of them, her heart and emotions in a turmoil. She felt warm all over at Mack's words. Then she chilled with her next thought. How could a former marine care for a Russian spy?

And as the miles ticked away, she prayed they'd find Toby and free him from his captor. Anything beyond that goal could wait to be resolved. Toby came first.

Chapter Twelve

Mack switched off the lights as they neared the location of the lake cabin. Half a mile away, he pulled the car to a stop and shut off the engine. He checked the weapon he wore beneath his jacket and opened the door to get out.

"Why are we stopping?" Riley got out of the car and stood beside Mack.

"We'll go the rest of the way on foot. That way, Pruett won't know we're there before we get to the door. If he has the boy, he won't have time to hide him." He shot a glance her way in the light from the stars overhead. "Ready?"

Riley nodded.

They followed the road, checking numbers on the mailboxes as they went until they neared Pruett's. From the road, they couldn't see anything but a dim light in the woods, along a rutted gravel road that led in.

Abandoning the road, Riley and Mack entered the woods, moving in the deep shadows of the tree canopy, with limited patches of starlight to guide them as they walked parallel to the gravel road. Soon the cabin appeared in a clearing, a single light shining through a window.

When Riley started forward, Mack held out a hand to stop her. "Let me go first." Pruett might be an engineer and a desk jockey, but he also might understand booby traps and how to set them.

Easing forward, Mack checked for trip wires and security cameras. When he found none, he waved Riley forward.

The cabin stood on piers, the windows a little higher than eye level unless one was to climb up on the porch. Since the porch would expose them too much, Mack ruled that out.

"You'll have to look," Mack whispered. He bent his long body, squatting low. "Climb on my shoulders."

Riley gave him a hesitant look. "Are you sure?"

He nodded and jerked his thumb toward his back. "Hop on. You'll be able to see into the window. Be careful no one sees you."

Riley slipped her legs over his shoulders and rested her hands on his head.

Mack straightened and, holding on to her thighs, shifted sideways toward the window.

"Stop," Riley said softly, her fingers curling into his hair.

He liked the warmth of her legs around his neck and the way her fingers feathered through his hair. But they were there to find Toby. "See anything?" Mack said, his voice barely above a whisper.

"Not yet." She leaned a little to her left. "Wait. I see someone lying on the couch."

"Pruett?"

"I can't tell," Riley said.

"What's he doing?"

"I can't tell," she said. "He's not moving."

"Not moving asleep?" Mack asked. "Or not moving dead?"

"Uh…" She leaned a little farther to the left. "I don't know."

Mack didn't like that he couldn't see in, but Riley couldn't lift him up. "Any sign of Toby?"

Her body seemed to sag. "No."

"Hold on, we're moving around to another window." Mack walked with Riley on his shoulders around to another window at the back of the cabin. The ground sloped toward the lake, making the window even higher from their level. "Can you see inside?"

"This is a bedroom." Riley leaned forward, pressing her hands on top of his head. "It's dark in the room. I can't see much, but I don't think Toby's in there."

"Moving." Mack moved to the next window.

"Another bedroom. I can't see Toby," she said, her voice flat, disappointed.

The next window proved to be the kitchen and again, no Toby.

Riley tugged at his hair. "Let me down."

Mack bent to a squat.

Riley dropped to the ground. "I'm going in."

"What if he's armed?" Mack asked.

"You're armed. You can shoot him."

Mack shook his head. "I'd be trespassing on his property. He'd have every right to shoot me first."

"Then we'll ask him to let us in. No guns necessary. We'll be stranded on the road because our car broke down."

"And he'll believe his coworker just happened to be in the neighborhood?"

"If Steve's got Toby, I'll shoot him myself. We won't need an excuse." Riley turned toward the porch. "Stay here. It might get sticky."

"I'm coming."

"Suit yourself." Riley marched up the steps and knocked on the door.

Mack followed, just as determined to find Toby as

Riley, and even more determined to keep her from getting herself killed.

Mack tugged Riley to the side of the door. If Pruett had a gun and started shooting, he'd aim for the door and the person standing on the other side. The wall gave a little bit of cover. Not much, but at least out of the direct line of fire.

The sound of feet hitting the floor came to them, and then footsteps leading toward the back of the house.

"He's heading for the back door," Riley said. She leaped off the porch and raced around to the back of the house.

Mack struggled to keep up, afraid Pruett would be desperate and try to hurt Riley.

Riley had just reached the back porch when Mack ran around the corner.

A man burst through the rear entry, flinging the door open so hard it hit the wall.

Before he could reach Riley, she ran up the steps and planted herself in front of the man.

"Hello, Steve," Riley said, her tone even, dangerous.

"Riley," Pruett said. "What are you doing here?"

"I thought you might be able to help me."

Pruett tried to go around her, but Riley stepped in his path. "Going somewhere?"

"I think I left the stove on at my house in the city," he said.

"Yeah?" Riley snorted. "Well, I can tell you that you didn't."

"But I did. I need to get there and turn it off before the house catches fire."

"The stove isn't on, and the house isn't going to catch fire." Riley stepped closer to Pruett. "But maybe we should check inside your cabin and see if the stove is on here." She stepped closer to Pruett.

Mack climbed the porch steps. "Right. Perhaps you need to show us your stove."

Pruett's eyes widened when Mack stepped up behind Riley. He backed up, and his brow furrowed. "My stove isn't on here. I'm going to have to ask you to leave."

Riley shook her head and advanced on the man. "We're not leaving until we're certain your stove is off."

Pruett edged toward the door. "You're not invited into my cabin."

Riley's eyes narrowed. "I think we are."

"I'll call the p-police," Pruett stuttered, not sounding at all convincing.

"Go ahead." Riley walked up to the man and poked a finger at his chest. "Call the police."

The man's gaze shifted from Riley to Mack and

back to Riley. He dived for the door and slammed it closed.

Mack reached the door before the man could lock it. He twisted the knob and applied a muscled shoulder to the paneled wood.

The door slammed open, shoving Pruett backward. He staggered until his back hit a wall. "You're t-trespassing," he said. "You can't come in."

"Yes. We can." Mack barged in and towered over the engineer. "Unless you think you can make me leave."

RILEY ALMOST LAUGHED at the way Pruett cowered under Mack's glare.

"Why don't you want to let us in, Steve?" She walked past Pruett into the kitchen. Everything had a place in the neat little kitchen, and everything was in its place. "Do you have something to hide?" She pushed the stainless steel toaster from one position to another, leaving a fingerprint on the steel, and moved on.

Steve squeezed around Mack and hurried after Riley. "No. No. I have nothing to hide." He moved the toaster back to its original position and used a paper towel to wipe the print off.

"Nothing at all?" Riley opened a cabinet door where glasses were lined up neatly, and pulled out a tumbler. She walked to the refrigerator and took out a bottle of orange juice, sluiced it into the cup, spilling a couple of drops on the countertop. "You don't mind if I help myself to a drink, do you?"

Pruett stared at the drops of juice on the countertop. "No. Help yourself and then leave."

"Why are you in such a hurry to see us leave? I'd think it would be lonely out here all by yourself." Riley drank the juice and set the glass on the counter. "Are you by yourself, Steve?" She moved toward the hallway leading to the bedrooms, searching for any doors she couldn't see from outside the house. Could the man be hiding Toby in a closet?

"Of c-course I'm alone." Steve lifted the glass, placed it in the sink and wiped the counter with a paper towel.

"All alone?" Riley said as she headed down the hallway to the two bedrooms. Her heart sped as she neared the first one and flipped the light switch. A dull yellow light illuminated the room. A dark walnut bed stood against one wall, covered in a neat, solid gray comforter and white pillows.

Riley checked beneath the bed and in the closet, searching for any sign of Toby or of a hidden door. The closet contained exactly five hangers with jeans on two, two button-down white shirts and a winter coat zipped from hem to neck.

Abandoning the room, Riley hurried to the next room where a white iron bed was pushed against the wall and covered in a blue-and-white quilt, trimmed in red. Pillows were stacked neatly against the headboard, and a small lamp stood on a nightstand beside the bed. Riley checked in the closet, starting to get worried they wouldn't find anything and tired of playing games with Pruett, when all she wanted was her brother.

The closet was empty, except for a box fan. When she bent to look beneath the bed, a small swath of fabric caught her eye near the wall by the headboard. She reached beneath the box spring and snagged a garment and pulled it out into the open. Her heart sank into the pit of her belly and then rose to choke the air out of her throat. She held a small hoodie in her fist, her hand shaking as she stared at the dinosaur on the front left side.

She turned with the garment in her hand, her gaze shooting to Pruett. "Where did you get this?" she demanded.

Pruett's eyes widened, and he dived for the front living area.

Mack was faster, catching the man by the back of his collar before he could get through the front door. Holding him easily by his shirt, Mack walked Pruett back to stand in front of Riley. "Answer her," he commanded.

Pruett's face paled. "I don't know."

"Wrong answer," Riley said. "Try again."

"It must have been there since I bought the house," the engineer said.

Riley shook her head and glared at the man. "Where's Toby?" She took a step toward Pruett and got in his face. Her lips peeled back in a vicious sneer. "Where's my brother?"

Pruett held up his hands "I don't know what you're talking about. I didn't even know you had a brother."

Riley shoved the jacket into the man's face. "Don't lie to me. This is Toby's jacket. Where is he?" Her hand and her voice shook with her rage.

Mack grabbed Pruett's arm and yanked it up behind his back, pushing it high between his shoulder blades. "Are you going to tell us where the boy is, or am I going to have to hurt you?"

Riley wanted to be the one to inflict pain on her coworker. "Just tell us where he is and we'll leave you alone."

Pruett's face screwed up in pain. "Ow, ow. You're going to break my arm." He danced up on his toes, trying to relieve the pressure on his arm.

"That's not all I'm going to break." Mack pushed the arm up higher.

"Okay. Okay. I'll tell you what I know," the man cried.

Mack backed off on the pressure but didn't release the wrist he held behind Pruett's back.

Riley crossed her arms over her chest, her heart

pounding, her attention on the man standing in front of her. Finally, she'd find Toby.

Pruett looked at the jacket and glared. "Damned kid did nothing but cry."

Riley reached out and slapped Pruett's face. "Bastard! He was probably frightened out of his mind. Where is my brother?"

"I gave him to that woman."

"What woman?" By this time, Riley was so frustrated she could have shaken Pruett until his teeth rattled. "Where is she?"

"At her home in the Arlington slums with her own brats. I should never have gotten involved in this. She said it would be easy money. All I had to do was take the kid. I didn't know I'd be babysitting the brat."

Grinding her back teeth, Riley fought to keep from pounding her fist into Pruett's face. "What woman? Does she have a name?"

"Bridgett, the night cleaning woman."

Riley's head jerked up. "Bridgett? She had you take Toby?"

"She paid the loan shark to get him off my back. In return, all I had to do was get the kid and deliver him to her. She didn't tell me I'd have to hold him overnight. I don't even like kids."

"Where does Bridgett live?" Riley asked, her tone tight, her fists tighter.

He rattled off the address and jerked his head toward Mack. "Now call off your Neanderthal."

"I ought to let him break every bone in your body for kidnapping a little boy. You had no right to take him."

"Good grief." Pruett sneered. "It's not like I hurt him or anything. I slipped through his window, picked him up while he was sleeping and left. It wasn't until he woke up that he started screaming."

Riley slammed her fist into Pruett's gut, her anger making her see red. "I hope you rot in hell." She strode past Mack and Pruett, rubbing her bruised knuckles. "Come on, Mack."

"What do you want me to do with him?" he asked.

"Bring him. We can't have him warning Bridgett."

"We can drop him off with one of the guys," Mack suggested.

"Yeah," Riley agreed. "And once we find Toby, we'll file charges and have him hauled off to jail."

"She swore she wouldn't hurt the boy," Pruett said. "I wouldn't have taken him otherwise."

"Shut up," Riley said without looking back at the man. "There's no excuse for stealing a child from his home. None."

"Why did she want him?" Mack asked.

"She said she was worried, and she was going

to take him to a better place to live. I needed the money—she offered to pay off my debt. How was I to know he was related to Ms. Lansing?"

Riley didn't slow as she pushed through the front door and out onto the porch. She couldn't believe the man could be so callous about abducting a little boy. "It doesn't matter who he was related to. You had no right to take him." She dropped down off the porch and turned to Mack. "I'll get the car."

He nodded. "The keys are in the ignition."

Riley jogged away, taking the road instead of cutting through the woods. Her heart hurt for Toby. The child had to be so confused and scared. She ran all the way back to her car, dived into the driver's seat and pulled up to the house.

"Pruett and I will ride in the back seat, if you don't mind driving," Mack said. "I called Declan. He's sending Gus to meet us at an exit close to where we're going. He'll take care of Pruett until we can find Toby." Mack shoved Pruett into the back seat and slipped in beside him. "Make any stupid moves, and I'll make sure you regret it."

Pruett shook his head, rubbing his arm. "I'm done with all this. Find the kid so I can get on with my life."

"Declan's getting quite the collection going," Riley muttered. "Does he have sufficient staff?" She met Mack's gaze in the mirror.

Mack's jaw tightened. "He'll have to."

Riley pulled away from the house, bumping along the gravel to the main road. As soon the tires hit pavement, she laid her foot to the accelerator and raced back to Arlington.

Within thirty minutes, she'd dropped Pruett with Gus, Mack had moved up to the passenger seat, and they'd driven to within a couple blocks of Bridgett's house. As before, they parked two blocks away and walked the rest of the way to the address.

The building was a small cottage on a street full of similar small houses with peeling paint, sagging eaves and broken bicycles scattered across the small yards. Its windows had been blacked out, and no movement could be detected from within.

Riley and Mack circled the house, searching for any sign of occupancy. Finally, Riley shrugged, walked up to the front door and knocked.

A child's cry sounded from inside.

Riley gripped the door handle, twisted the knob and pushed as hard as she could. The door was locked. She pulled her file from her back pocket and fit it in the keyhole. Her hands shaking, she worked to unlock the door, not knowing whether the child who'd cried had been Toby or one of the janitor's. It didn't matter. If there was even a small chance it was Toby, she had to get to him before anyone hurt him.

The lock clicked and the knob turned.

"Stay low." Mack pushed past her, entering the residence, his handgun drawn.

Riley ducked down, hurried through the door and hugged the shadows. The lights had been turned off, but a dull glow came from a night-light close to the floor.

They entered a living area strewn with ragged blankets on the couches, battered toys littering the floor and dirty dishes lying on boxes used as end tables.

Nothing moved, and there was no sign of the people who'd created the mess.

Mack eased down a hallway, passing the entrance to a small, dirty kitchen with sippy cups, plastic plates with half-eaten dinners, and dirty pans scattered across the counter, as if someone had interrupted a family's meal.

A door clicked shut in another room in the small house. The sound of a sob came from down the hallway.

Riley started in that direction, but Mack quickly passed her and reach the next doorway before she could.

Mack eased open the door to a small bedroom.

A gasp and a whimper made Riley peek over Mack's shoulder.

Crowded in the corner, huddled close to the floor,

were the janitorial aide, Bridgett, three small children and Toby.

"Toby!" Riley cried out, and pushed past Mack.

Her brother glanced up at her, his eyes wide, dark circles smudged beneath them. "Riley?" Tears slipped down his cheeks as he staggered to his feet and raced into her arms.

Riley scooped him up and hugged him close to her chest.

Mack stood over her, his gun pointed at the woman still huddled on the floor with the three small children.

"Please, don't hurt us," she said, tears welling in her eyes. "I didn't want to do it. But they made me." Her bottom lip trembled and her body shook with a silent sob.

"Do what? And who made you do it?" Mack asked.

"A woman and two men." Bridgett clutched her children closer. "They said they'd turn me in for stealing supplies from Quest."

"Why didn't you tell someone?" Mack asked. "Surely they would've understood."

"I was afraid. I didn't want to go to jail. Even if I didn't go to jail, they'd take my children away. My babies would have no one." She buried her face in the dark hair of a pretty toddler who wore pink pajamas and had a smear of cheese across her cheek.

"They would split my children up and send them to foster homes. My children would not know their siblings. I wouldn't be there to protect them."

Riley held Toby, listening to Bridgett's story. She didn't care. She had her brother in her embrace, and that was all that mattered.

Toby's little arms wrapped around her neck in a stranglehold. After a long, hard hug, Riley pushed him to arm's length and studied him from head to toe. She brushed a lock of his hair away from his forehead and gave him a watery smile. "Are you okay?"

He nodded and flung his arms around her neck again, holding tightly as if he would never let go.

Riley laughed, the sound catching on a sob. When she turned to look up at Mack, a shadow fell over the doorway. Her heart leaped into her throat. As she opened her mouth to scream, a hand swung out with a dark stick and hit Mack in the back of the head.

Mack staggered and dropped to his knees.

A large man in dark clothing and a dark ski mask stepped through the door and hit Mack in the head again.

Riley pushed Toby behind her and jumped to her feet. Before the man with a stick could hit Mack again, she kicked the man's wrist, knocking the stick loose, sending it flying across the room.

As she cocked her leg to kick again, another figure entered the room also wearing dark clothes and a ski mask.

This man caught her around the waist and clamped a meaty hand over her mouth. She fought, elbowing him in the gut and stomping his instep, but the hand over her mouth also held a cloth with sweet-smelling perfume.

Within seconds, the fight leached out of Riley. Her muscles refused to cooperate, and she went limp in the man's arms. Darkness consumed her. Her last sight was of Mack, lying motionless against the floor.

Chapter Thirteen

Mack fought the darkness, pushing through a gray haze to get to Riley. Every time he thought he'd make it, he slipped back into the abyss. Someone threatened Riley. She was in trouble. He couldn't just lie there and let her be taken or harmed.

Again, he pushed through the thick gray cloud and blinked open his eyes. Gloom still surrounded him.

The murmur of voices let him know the dimness wasn't from unconsciousness, but the lack of light in the room where he lay with his face on a hard surface.

"Mama, is the man dead?" a child's voice asked.

"I don't know," a woman's voice responded.

Then a soft hand brushed across his brow and reached down to touch the base of his throat. "He's still alive," she said. "Get my cell phone."

The patter of bare little feet sounded on the floor, passing by Mack's head. He could see the shadow of a very small child inching past him to the open doorway.

Mack shifted his hands beneath himself and pushed his body up to a sitting position. His vision blurred, and he nearly threw up.

"Mister, you should lie down until I can call an ambulance. You could have a brain or spine injury. Movement could make it worse."

He turned his head to see the woman named Bridgett kneeling beside him. The movement made his head swim and his vision fade. Forcing himself to stay awake and alert, he moved his head more slowly, taking in the room, the bed, two very small children and the sound of another moving about the house.

"Where's Riley?" he asked, his voice gravelly, his tongue feeling like he'd swallowed a wad of cotton. He frowned. "And Toby. Where's the boy?"

Bridgett's forehead wrinkled and her eyes filled. "They took Miss Lansing and the boy."

"Where?"

"I don't know." She wrung her hands.

"Why didn't you try to stop them?" As soon as he said the words, he knew they were stupid and spoken in anger. Not anger at Bridgett, but at himself for not anticipating the attack or hearing their approach.

"They told me if I interfered, they'd kill me." Bridgett held open her arms as the oldest of her daughters ran back into the room carrying a cell phone.

Bridgett wrapped the child in the curve of one arm while she took the cell phone in the other hand. "I'm calling for an ambulance and the police."

"Don't do it for me. I'll be gone before they get here." He bent forward, dragged his feet beneath himself and stood. As soon as he was upright, he swayed and staggered a few steps. He braced his hand against the wall and waited for the dizziness to pass.

"Sir, you should sit until the EMTs arrive," Bridgett said. "You could have a concussion."

"I can't sit. The more time that passes, the farther away they will get with Riley and Toby." He pulled his own cell phone out of his pocket and hit the number for Declan.

Declan answered after the first ring. "Mack, where are you?"

Mack touched the back of his head and winced. "I'm at the house of the woman who performs janitorial services at Quest. She had Riley's brother. We were attacked, and now they have Riley and Toby. Get Jonah on that GPS tracker and find Riley. Did Pruett have anything else to say? Was his only contact Bridgett with the cleaning service?"

"He confessed to making the call to Riley so that she could hear her brother's voice. But he swears he only ever had contact with Bridgett."

"And do you believe him?" Mack asked.

"He sounded legit." Declan chuckled. "And Gus might have scared him a little."

Mack's lips curled slightly as he imagined Gus getting in the overwrought engineer's face. Then his jaw tightened. "We need the names of the people who forced Bridgett and Pruett to do what they did. More than that, I need directions to where they've taken Riley and the kid."

"Working on that," Declan said. "Jonah's on it. As soon as he's got her in his sights, we'll feed you the information. He's also been busy going through all the people Riley has had immediate contact with. We're not getting much of anything."

"What about the nanny?" Mack asked.

"We searched on her name and traced her back to where she lived next door to Riley's home when she was growing up. Margaret Weems moved in at the same time as the Lansings. We didn't find any other information on her previous residence. It was a dead end."

Too many dead ends.

"I'm heading for the car. As soon as you get a bead on Riley, call." He ended the call and glanced at Bridgett. "Are you going to be all right?"

She gathered her children around her and nodded. "I didn't want to do it, but I'm going to my mother's house in Raleigh tonight. I don't feel safe here."

"Good. In the meantime, lock your doors."

Bridgett shook her head. "That didn't do much good for me. You were able to get in."

"True. Take what you need and leave as soon as possible." He headed for the door.

Bridgett reached out and touched his arm. "Are you going to tell the management at Quest I took some of their supplies?"

"I'm not," he said.

Bridgett drew in a deep breath. "I'll purchase the toilet paper I took and return it. I can't afford to lose my job over three rolls of toilet paper. I just couldn't afford to buy any, what with the cost of child care taking most of my paycheck."

Mack felt for the woman but couldn't afford to stick around, not with Riley in danger. He dug in his pocket and pulled out a business card and a wad of cash. He pressed them into her hand. "Take the money, get the kids to a hotel room and call this number in a couple days. Mrs. Halverson might be able to help you."

Bridgett pushed the money back at him. "I can't take your money. I shouldn't have taken the supplies. I'm responsible for my actions and my children. I'll do what's right."

Mack curled her fingers around the money and card. "We all need a little help sometimes. Keep it."

He didn't give her the opportunity to hand it back a second time. Mack left her house and ran the two blocks to Riley's vehicle. Once he was inside and had switched on the engine, his cell phone rang.

"We have her on the tracking program," Declan said. "You're on speaker with Jonah."

"Give me the directions," Mack said as he whipped the car out onto the road.

"Head into downtown DC."

WATER SPLASHED ONTO her face brought Riley to consciousness. She snorted some up her nose and coughed. When she tried to raise her hands to push the wet hair out of her face, she couldn't move her arms.

She looked down at where her wrists were duct-taped to the arms of a utilitarian metal office chair. For a moment, her brain couldn't grasp what was happening. Her gaze shot around the room, taking in the concrete block walls of what appeared to be a basement lit by a single dull yellow light hanging by a cord from the ceiling.

Riley's pulse skittered in her veins, and her gut knotted. She pulled at the tape binding her wrists to the chair.

"You didn't think you could lie to us and get

away with it, did you?" a deep male voice said from behind her.

A man circled her. He wore dark pants, a dark shirt and a fedora pulled low over the bridge of his nose. The minimal lighting cast a deep shadow over his face.

Riley couldn't tell who he was, nor did she recognize his voice. She could sense the danger in the way he walked and tapped a metal rod against the palm of his hand.

He hit a switch on the metal rod and touched it to her bare skin.

A jolt of electricity blasted through her.

Riley screamed, the pain so blinding it nearly made her pass out. She dragged in a breath, fighting to remain calm. "Where is my brother?"

The man tapped the wand against his palm again. "You will never see your brother again."

"Like hell I won't." Riley jerked against her bindings. She planted her feet against the floor and tried to rise, chair and all.

A strong hand clamped down on her shoulder, forcing her to see sit down.

"Charlotte Halverson lives." The man paced in front of her. "Your job was to kill her. Because you did not fulfill your duties, your brother is lost to you forever."

Riley sat silently, anger burning deep inside. She

refused to believe she would never see Toby again. If it were the last thing she ever did, she'd find her brother and kill the people who stole him from her.

"Do you know what we do with agents who are not loyal to the mother country?" He smiled, his lips parting in a feral grin. "Some would think that we would kill the agent." The man snorted. "That would be too easy. We do not waste years of training without first attempting to re-assimilate the protégé back into the fold."

He paced several steps in front of her, turned and paced back the way he had come, all the while tapping the rod against his palm.

Riley tried to memorize the contours of the man's face and commit them to her memory for when she would track him down and kill him. But after a few minutes of watching him pace, she shifted to the rod in his hand, knowing what pain it could inflict.

The man in black stopped in front of her and barked out, "Who do you work for?"

Riley bit down hard on her tongue to keep from answering.

The wand shot out and bit into her arm, sending a shock of electricity through her body.

Riley clamped her jaw tight, refusing to even whimper, though the pain was excruciating.

His eyes narrowing, the man in the fedora leaned closer, his fetid breath making Riley gag. "You will learn the proper response to that question." He raised the wand again.

Riley dug her feet into the concrete floor, jerked forward and rammed her head into the man's chest, knocking him backward several feet.

The fedora remained in place even though the man staggered, tripped and fell, landing hard on his backside.

Again, a hand clamped on her shoulder, shoving her back in her seat and the chair legs back to the floor.

She landed with a jolt that rattled her teeth.

Once the man on the floor rose, he hit her again with the electric prod.

Electricity shot through her entire body.

He held the prod against her arm so long the pain caused her system to shut down. Darkness became her friend.

MINUTES, MAYBE HOURS later, Riley awoke to someone tugging at the tape on her wrists.

When she opened her eyes, Riley stared into the eyes of Margaret Weems, her nanny.

"You won't have much time," the woman said.

"Margaret?" Riley blinked and stared around the room. "Why...how did you find me?"

"I can't explain now," she said. "Toby is in a

room down the hall. You have to leave now, before they come back."

"Before who comes back?" Riley shook her head. Then the images she'd thought were just a nightmare came back to her. "You need to get out of here. Go," she insisted. "If they catch you, they'll torture you."

"You think I don't know that?" She cut away at the tape on Riley's right wrist, freeing her hand from the chair. Then she rounded to the other side and slipped the blade of a knife beneath the other band of duct tape and ripped through it as well.

Riley rose from the chair and peeled the rest of the tape from her wrists, taking a layer of skin with it.

"You have to hurry," Margaret urged. "They will be back soon."

"I'm not leaving without you." Riley hooked the woman's arm and half dragged her toward the door.

Margaret set her feet into the concrete and yanked her arm free of Riley's hold. "Go without me. I will only slow down you and Toby."

"But they will kill you."

"My job here is done." Margaret stepped backward. "It is time for you to make your own decisions about who you are and what you believe in."

Riley shook her head, her eyes narrowing. "What do you mean?"

"I was there when you were born. I worked alongside your parents when you got your training." She lifted her chin. "I knew what they had planned for you, yet I still didn't stop it from happening. It was my job to protect you and your brother until such a time when they would call you to duty."

"What are you talking about?" Riley stared at the woman as if for the first time. She'd known Margaret all her life. The woman was like the grandmother she never had. Riley trusted her with her life, and more importantly, Toby's life.

Margaret's gaze shot toward the door. "You need to leave now."

"You need to come with me," Riley said.

"No," she said, "my job is done. They will hunt me down for releasing you." She shook her head, the lines around her eyes and mouth seeming so much deeper. "I don't have the strength to run."

Riley's chest squeezed tightly. "I don't know what you've done, or what role you played in kidnapping my brother. But I won't let them hurt you."

Margaret held up her hand with a small pill pinched between her fingers. "They won't hurt me," she said with a smile, and slipped the pill beneath her tongue.

Riley leaped toward the woman, but she was too late.

Margaret dropped to her knees and slumped to the floor. She coughed twice, and foam bubbled from her mouth.

"Holy hell, Margaret." Riley knelt beside her. "Spit it out."

Margaret shook her head and raised her hand. "Take my ring."

"No, Margaret, you wear it." Riley held the woman's hand and stared down into her eyes.

Margaret coughed again. "Take the ring. It has meaning. Find it, and you will know what to do." Her last words faded into silence, and all tension left her body.

Riley pressed her fingers to the base of Margaret's throat, searching for a pulse. There was none. Her nanny, and her old friend, was dead.

As she released Margaret's hand, she felt the cool metal of the ring Margaret had wanted her to take. She recognized it as one Margaret had always worn on her right hand. It was made of yellow gold, white gold and rose gold bands twisted together. The ring had seemed very important to Margaret. What she meant about finding the meaning of the ring made no sense to Riley. She didn't have time to work through the riddle. Instead, she slipped it from Margaret's finger and pushed it into the pocket of her jeans.

The sound of footsteps alerted her to people moving in the hallway outside the door.

Riley dived behind the door as it opened.

A large man dressed in black, wearing a black ski mask, stepped into the room and nearly tripped over Margaret's body. As he bent toward the woman on the floor, Riley balled both fists together and hit the man in the side of the head as hard as she could.

The big man fell over on his side.

Before he could rise, Riley kicked him in the face, breaking his nose.

The man yelled, his eyes teared, and he grabbed his face and hunched over.

Riley dived past him into the hallway. She didn't know which door hid Toby, but she vowed to find him and free him before these monsters tortured him as well.

Chapter Fourteen

"You should be within a block of the building where she's being held," Jonah's voice said from the speaker on Mack's cell phone.

"Mack?" a female voice came across. "This is Grace."

He recognized Grace's voice. "Where's Declan?" Mack asked.

"He's on his way," Grace said. "He has Gus, Mustang and Snow with him."

"What's his ETA?" Mack asked as he pulled Riley's car over to the side of the road.

"They should be right behind you," Jonah answered. "I have them up on the GPS as well." Jonah gave him the address of the building in which he'd find Riley.

Committing the name and numbers to memory,

Mack turned to see headlights heading his way. His grabbed his cell phone, switched it to silent and waited for the other members of his team to climb out of Declan's truck.

Declan hurried toward him, carrying a handgun in one hand and a heavy flashlight in the other.

"Who's guarding Charlie?" Mack asked.

"Seems since the cat was out of the bag, she'd be safer at her own house," Declan said. "Cole and Mustang sneaked her out of the hospital on a gurney and into the back of a laundry truck. They got her back to her house and its state-of-the-art security system. Cole and Jonah are with her. We thought you might need a little help here."

Mack nodded. "I'm guessing there were at least two guys who jumped us. There might be more where we're heading." His fists clenched. "Those two guys should never have surprised me like that."

"Don't beat yourself up," Declan said. "The main focus now is finding Riley and getting her and her brother back."

"Agreed. Let's do this." Mack took the lead, determined to find Riley and end the threat to her and her brother.

Declan, Mustang, Snow and Gus fell in behind him. Their training as Force Recon marines kicked in and they moved from shadow to shadow, closing in on what appeared to be an abandoned building that might have been a small factory or machine shop.

When they came within spitting distance, Mack held up his fist.

The team stopped in place. Declan moved up in line with Mack.

"See the broken window near the right corner of the rear of the building?" Mack pointed. The window was high enough off the ground that they wouldn't be able to just look inside.

Declan nodded. "I'll give you a boost so you can make a quick assessment."

Mustang and Gus split off and circled to the other side of the building. Snow provided cover should someone discover Mack and Declan while they were exposed, attempting to get a look inside.

Mack checked left and then right before he ran for the building. Declan ran with him. As soon as they reached the wall below the broken window, Declan bent over. Mack stepped up on his back and pulled himself up to the window.

Inside the structure was old machinery covered in dust and dirt. The place looked like it hadn't been occupied for at least ten, maybe fifteen years. What was unusual was that in a far corner there was a dull light over a doorway. Mack would have assumed all electricity had long since been shut off.

Mack dropped back to the ground.

"See anyone?" Declan asked.

"No."

Moments later, Gus and Mustang returned from their reconnaissance of the rest of the outside of the building.

"There are three entrances," Mustang said. "One is on the front of the building. It's a huge double door that has been boarded up. There's a side door that was probably used for employee entrance and a loading dock at the rear."

"Which entrance do you suggest?" Mack asked.

"The rear dock," Gus reported.

"Did you see any guards posted?"

Gus shook his head. "Not one."

"That doesn't make me feel confident," Mack said. "They could be lying in wait in the shadows. We'll have to be careful breaching the building."

The men set off, following the shadowy exterior of the neighboring building until they reached the back corner of the old manufacturing business.

Then, one by one, they ran across to the loading dock.

Mack found a door near the truck loading area. The door wasn't locked, nor was it dusty like the rest of the interior appeared. He twisted the knob slowly and eased the door open.

Inside and to the left was a chair with a guard seated in it, his head tipped back, resting against the wall. The man was half asleep, if not completely out. And he had a military-grade rifle lying across his lap.

Mack eased up to him, grabbed the rifle and hit him in the head with the butt of his own weapon.

The man slumped over and fell to the floor.

Declan pulled zip ties out of his back pocket, then secured the guard's wrists and ankles and slapped a piece of duct tape over his mouth.

"Where'd you get the tape?" Mack asked.

Declan chuckled softly. "I always bring a little bit in my pocket. It can fix anything."

They checked the immediate vicinity for more guards but didn't find any. Declan waved the other two men into the building and they spread out, searching the main floor for offices or rooms in which they might have hidden Riley and Toby.

They came up empty as they worked their way past large rusting machinery to the other end of the building and the door with the light glowing over it.

Mack reached the door first and stepped through, holding his pistol in front of him. The door was a stairwell leading downward into a basement. The dirty yellow light was barely bright enough to illuminate the stairs. Mack tiptoed downward into the bowels of the building. Near the bottom of the staircase were two guards standing on either side of a broad hallway.

They didn't see Mack coming because they were looking down the hallway.

Footsteps sounded on the filthy concrete floors.

Mack's attention turned to what the two men were staring at.

A figure ran into one of the rooms off the hallway.

The men spoke to each other in Russian. One of them left his post and ran after the figure.

Mack slipped up behind the other man and grabbed him around the throat in a headlock. He squeezed hard, cutting off the man's air. He held him tightly in a stranglehold.

The man was large but unable to break free of Mack's grip. Soon, he went limp from lack of oxygen. Once again, Declan pulled out the zip ties and secured the man's wrists and ankles. Then he pressed duct tape over his mouth and dragged him into an empty room to the man's left. Already, the guy had regained consciousness and was fighting mad, making grunting noises in an attempt to capture the attention of other members of his group in the building.

Mack didn't wait for Declan and the others. He figured they didn't have much time before others discovered they were there. They had to find Riley and Toby soon.

The sound of a struggle drew Mack's attention. The figure that had disappeared into the room down the hallway had been smaller, not bulky like the guards. The thought that it might be Riley had him running down the hallway.

Another door burst open in front of him and three burly men dressed in black barreled through. A shout went out from the lead man.

Mack didn't have time to do more than react. He ducked low and plowed into the first guy, hitting him square in the gut, sending him flying backward into one of the others. The two men fell in a heap on the floor and scrambled to untangle themselves.

The third man stepped aside, letting his comrades crash without taking him down with them. He threw a meaty fist toward Mack.

Mack twisted sideways.

The fist missed his face and rammed into his shoulder, jerking him around.

Mack staggered backward, righted himself and went after the man.

A gun appeared in the man's hand.

Adrenaline firing through his veins, Mack didn't slow. He sent a side kick into his wrist. The gun went off before it flew from the man's hand and hit the floor, skittering out of reach.

The bullet hit the wall beside Mack.

He didn't care. As long as he could keep moving, he would.

Sounds of struggles and a muffled scream came from the doorway down the hall. Riley needed him.

He was certain. One man in the way wouldn't keep Mack from reaching her.

He swung his fist, catching the man in the chin, sending him slamming back against the wall behind him.

Gunfire went off behind him, but Mack couldn't shift his attention from the man in front of him. Cocking his leg, he shot a powerful kick into the man's thigh.

The distinct sound of a bone snapping echoed off the concrete block walls. Mack's opponent dropped to the floor.

Declan was there with zip ties to keep the man immobile.

Together they secured the other two men and all their weapons.

With the acrid scent of gunpowder still stinging Mack's nostrils, he jogged toward the doorway where the guard had followed the slim figure inside.

Grunts and thumps sounded from within.

"Leave my brother alone," Riley's voice sounded.

His heart racing, Mack pushed through the door to find Riley in the clutches of one man, while another held Toby around the waist like a quarterback carrying a football.

The boy kicked and fought as hard as his little body could. "Let go of my sister!" he yelled.

Mack started for Riley but stopped short when he

noticed the gun in her captor's hand. The gun was pressed to Riley's temple.

"Don't worry about me," Riley said. "Help Toby."

"Move and I put a bullet through her head," said her captor, a large man with shaggy black hair and a rugged, pockmarked face. "And when she's dead, I'll kill the kid."

Riley stiffened, her fade hardening into a mask. She looked to Mack. Her eyes narrowed slightly and she gave the briefest of nods. Then she jabbed her elbow into the man's ribs and ducked out of his grip. The gun went off.

Mack's heart stopped for a moment.

But the bullet hit the wall instead of Riley's head. She broke free of her captor's grip, rounded behind him and kicked at the back of his legs. His knees buckled and he fell to the floor. Riley grabbed his wrist, the one holding the gun, and twisted it up behind his back. He held on as long as he could, until the gun fell from his grip and clattered to the floor.

A shout rose from the man holding Toby, and he dropped the boy to the floor. He shook his hand, where a bright red bite mark appeared.

Toby scrambled on all fours toward Mack.

The man who'd been holding him dived toward the kid, snagged his ankle and yanked him back.

Mack launched himself across the room and drove his fist into the man's face.

The thug released his hold on Toby and brought his fists up to defend himself against Mack's furious onslaught.

As he fought Toby's captor, he could see Riley in his peripheral vision. She'd jumped on the back of the man who'd threatened to kill her and her brother and held his arm tightly up between his shoulder blades.

Declan pushed through the door, scooped the boy up into his arms and handed him off to Mustang, who'd arrived behind him.

Mack threw a punch to his guy's gut.

The man doubled over as Mack brought up his knee, jamming it into his face. Then he grabbed the man's collar at the back of his neck and sent him flying behind Mack into Declan.

Declan sent the man facedown on the floor and planted a knee in his back.

Mack swung around, kicked the gun out of Riley's prisoner's reach and smiled down at her. "You make it hard for a man to save you."

She nodded. "I don't need a man to save me, but it's nice to know you could."

Declan cinched his guy's wrists with zip ties and handed a couple extras to Mack. He and Riley secured her prisoner and left him lying on the floor.

Mack helped Riley to her feet and into his arms.

Gus and Snow appeared in the doorway.

"The rest of the building is clear," Gus said.

"We found a body in another room. An older woman. No sign of struggle, but possibly poisoned. She had foam in her mouth."

Riley laid her head against Mack's chest. "The woman was Margaret Weems. My nanny."

"Your nanny?" Declan asked, his brow furrowed.

Riley nodded. "She was my handler." She shook her head. "I never knew. I thought she was the kind older woman who always lived next door to my parents. She was my surrogate grandmother. And when my parents died in that car wreck, it was natural for me to hire her as Toby's nanny."

Mack's chest tightened at the sorrow in Riley's face. "Who poisoned her?"

"She did it herself." Riley twisted a ring on her finger that hadn't been there before. "She helped me to escape. I think she was tired and wanted to go out on her own terms." She lifted her chin toward the men tied up on the floor. "They would have killed her anyway."

Mack brushed a strand of her hair back behind her ear. "Are you okay? Did they hurt you?"

Riley rubbed her hand over her arm. "I'm okay."

He could tell she wasn't, but he refused to argue. Not when they might still be in danger. "Let's call the police and get them to clean up this mess."

"Better yet, let's call the FBI," Riley said.

"Are you sure?" Mack asked. "We could get you

as far away from this as possible before we let them in on what's going on."

Riley shook her head. "No. I'm ready to face them. I've lived with this hanging over my head for so long, I need to deal with it, no matter the consequences."

Mustang entered the room, carrying Toby.

Riley smiled at the child and held open her arms. "Toby, sweetie. Everything is going to be all right."

The boy fell into her arms and buried his face against her neck. "I was scared."

"I know. So was I. But you were so brave." She kissed the top of his head. "Would you like to come live with me in the city?"

He lifted his head and stared into her face. "Yes, please." Toby kissed her cheek and wrapped his arms around her neck.

Mack's heart swelled at the love between the brother and sister. Riley would do anything for the kid. Even lay down her life for him.

She looked at him over Toby's head.

Mack held his arms open.

Riley stepped into them, still holding Toby. Mack wrapped them in his embrace and held them, praying he could do this for a lot longer. Maybe the rest of his life.

Declan stepped out of the building to get good cell phone reception to place a call to Charlie, who made the call to her contact in the FBI. Within twenty minutes, several unmarked vehicles arrived to process the scene in the abandoned factory.

Mack waited in fear of the FBI taking Riley prisoner and escorting her to an undisclosed location where they would interrogate her.

But they didn't. They thanked her for being an upstanding American citizen and doing the right thing, despite the odds stacked against her. She'd still have to answer questions, but she wasn't going to jail or a detention facility to be interrogated.

Two hours after the incident, Mack sat with Riley on a concrete step outside the old factory, with Toby asleep in his lap.

"What's going to happen from here?" he asked.

Riley shrugged. "I don't even know whether or not I'll be allowed to work at Quest anymore."

"Seems to me you're one of the most patriotic people in this country, despite what your parents and handler had in mind for you."

"You see it that way, but I doubt Quest will. They will learn that I was a trained Russian spy. They won't look beyond those words."

"My mother always told me, 'Don't borrow trouble.'" He slipped an arm around her shoulders. "You worked with the FBI to find out who was stealing secrets from Quest. Surely Quest will take that into account and let you stay on."

"I hope so. I'm Toby's only support. I need my job." She leaned into the curve of his arm. "What's going to happen to us? Now that I have Toby back, you'll move on to another assignment for Charlie."

"I'd like to see you still." Mack glanced down at the sleeping boy on his lap. "If you and Toby will have me around."

Riley wrapped her arm around Mack's waist. "I'd be sad if you didn't come around. I've been so busy being a provider and part-time parent to Toby, I forgot what it was like to be just me."

"I'd love to have the chance to learn who you are and be a part of Toby's life. I think my brother would have liked him. He's a fighter, this kid."

"Thank you for not giving up on us," Riley said. She leaned up in his arms and brushed her lips across his. "I think I could get used to having you around."

Mack's heart warmed. Surrounded by Riley and Toby, he'd never felt more complete. Since his own brother's death, he'd gone through life trying to prove to himself and the memory of Aiden that he was worthy of the life he'd been granted and that had been stolen from a little boy.

He didn't have to chase after that proof anymore.

But he vowed to be a part of Riley's and Toby's lives. And he would do his best to make sure they had the long, healthy lives they deserved.

Epilogue

Riley sat on the arm of the chair beside Mack in Charlie's living room. The team of Force Recon marines sat in a circle of sofas and chairs with Charlie at the head of the group.

Toby was in the kitchen with Charlie's chef, making cookies for all of them, happily chattering away to a master chef like he was his best buddy.

Riley rested her hand on Mack's shoulder. A week had passed since Margaret's death and the subsequent arrests of Steve Pruett, Tracy Gibson and the six men who'd been involved in Riley and Toby's abduction.

"I've worked with my contact in the FBI to clear Riley of all suspicion."

"Did you mention she'd been sent to assassinate you?"

"I did," Charlie said. "I also told them she didn't go through with it and never would. Riley is a true-blue American, despite her training as a Russian sleeper spy."

"And they bought it?" Riley asked.

Charlie nodded. "My dear husband wasn't the only one who had tight connections with the FBI. I have my own contacts, and they assured me you would have no trouble obtaining clearances and continuing your work in the Special Projects division at Quest."

Riley smiled. "Thank you, Mrs. Halverson. I was worried about how I'd provide for myself and my brother if I lost my job."

"Rest assured," Charlie said, "I also had a talk with one of the members of the board of directors at Quest. Though Steve Pruett, Tracy Gibson and Bridgett Paulson were arrested, I understand Ms. Paulson is out on bail to be with her children."

"Who offered to bail her out?" Mack asked. "I got the impression she didn't know anyone who could afford that kind of money."

Charlie shrugged. "I don't keep up with all the ins and outs of every investigation. I'm sure someone came up with the money. The poor woman was conscripted into the service of the Russians under duress. Like most women, she would do anything to protect her children, even set out electronic surveillance devices in her place of employment and pass on the orders and the packet of money to Steve Pruett to kidnap a child. She didn't know what was in that packet until Pruett dumped the boy in her lap."

"I'm surprised they let her out, and that they didn't take her children away from her," Riley said.

"I'm betting someone of influence had a lot to do with Ms. Paulson's bail being set low. She'll probably get off on her part in the kidnapping and the bugging of your office."

Charlie sighed. "She did, however, lose her job. But I have it on good authority she has an even better position that doesn't require her to work at night. She was able to place her children in a reputable day care and she'll be home with them every night."

"Again, I can't imagine who made that happen." Declan shook his head, his lips quirking upward.

Grace stood behind where he sat, her hand on his shoulder. "Charlie, you're too kind."

Again, Charlie shrugged. "What good is money if you can't help out other people less fortunate?"

"I'm glad Bridgett and her children won't suffer because of what happened. She was merely a pawn in a larger game." Absently, Riley twisted the ring on her finger. "I'm just sorry Margaret decided she'd had enough and took her own life." She stared down at the ring on her right hand. "She left me this ring with the strangest request."

Charlie's eyes narrowed. "What ring?"

Riley slipped the ring from her finger, crossed the room and held it out to the widow. "Her last wish was for me to look for the meaning of this ring and I'd know what to do." She shook her head. "I did a Google search on the ring and found the symbol to be a pattern called a trinity knot. The inscription inside the ring is in Russian."

"Can you read it?" Mack asked.

Riley snorted. "My parents were Russian, but in their effort to Americanize me, they refused to speak Russian in our house. I can't even read a word of Russian." She turned to Charlie to take the ring.

The older woman's face was pale, her eyes rounded, and the hand holding the ring shook. "I've seen this before. I know this ring."

Riley frowned. "Did you know Margaret?"

Charlie shook her head. "No. But I knew my husband. Or at least I thought I did." She took the ring and left the room, hurrying to another part of the house.

Riley frowned, her gaze following the widow until she disappeared down a hallway leading toward the master bedroom.

Mack stood and slipped an arm around her waist. "What do you make of her response?"

"I don't know what to make of it."

"Do you suppose Mr. Halverson knew Margaret?" Riley's roommate, Grace, asked.

Riley shrugged. "Apparently, there's a lot I didn't know about the woman I regarded as my surrogate grandmother. I thought she was just a nice old lady. Not a Russian sleeper spy handler. I wish she hadn't taken her life. I have a million questions I would have liked to ask her." She gave her roommate a sad smile. "I considered her a member of my family. She probably knew my parents even better than I did."

"She obviously cared about you and Toby, or she wouldn't have set you free in that basement," Mack noted.

"True. Now I'll never know the true extent of the underground spy movement."

"Perhaps the ring is a key to what more can be found," Grace suggested. "One of our classmates in college studied Russian. I think she went on to be a professor at one of the colleges here in the DC area. We could see if she can translate the inscription."

Riley nodded, wondering if Charlie would return the ring to her. The woman had been gone for several minutes with no sign of returning.

"What did you find out about the men in the factory basement?" Mack asked Declan.

"Charlie's contact in the FBI ran a background check and facial recognition software on them. They were Russians here on expired visas. They traced them back to connections with the Russian spy network. They were known for some pretty heinous torture treatments against the motherland enemies."

Riley shivered, her body remembering the shock of the electric cattle prod. She was very fortunate the marines had found her sooner rather than later. Though Margaret had helped her to escape, she wasn't so sure she'd have made it out alive if Mack and his team hadn't arrived when they did.

She leaned into the strength of his body, thankful he'd been Charlie's bodyguard at that gala. Riley truly believed fate had brought them together. And if at all possible, she hoped they could stay together for a very long time, getting to know each other better. Her body warmed at the thought of getting to know Mack's body better, knowing it would be a challenge with Toby living with her. But she was up for the challenge and couldn't imagine a life without her little brother.

Mack had been to her apartment several times since the incident in the old factory basement. Toby had taken to him immediately. Apparently, the boy had needed a strong male role model in his life.

Riley couldn't think of anyone who better fit that mold.

Moments later, Charlie reappeared with another ring. This one was bolder and broader. A more masculine version of the one Margaret had given Riley.

It had the trinity knot symbol on top and the same inscription inside, всегда и навсегда.

Jonah stepped forward. "We could enter the phrase in an online translator," he suggested.

Everyone in the living room followed him to the computer lab Mr. Halverson had constructed prior to his death.

Jonah sat at his keyboard, booted the computer and waited. When the monitor blinked to life, he quickly selected a translation application, switched the keyboard to Russian and keyed the letters of the inscription.

A second later, they had their answer.

Always and forever.

Riley shook her head. "I still don't know what it means. And I don't know what I'm supposed to do with it."

"I'll ask our classmate to research the rings and the inscription," Grace said. "Maybe she will come up with something more specific." She tapped her chin, and her brow lowered. "Come to think of it… I swear I saw something in one of the files I looked in when I was in your old boss's office at Quest. There was a file marked 'Trinity' in the cabinet in his office. I didn't think much of it then, but perhaps it has something to do with the ring, since it has the trinity knot on it."

Riley stared at her friend, her thoughts going beyond Grace's pretty face. "It's all too coincidental."

"I don't believe in coincidence," Mack said.

"I'd like to know what they all have to do with each other," Riley said. "I can visit Emily Monday morning when the university is open and I might find her in her office."

"You've had enough excitement for a lifetime. Why not let one of the others check into the rings?" Charlie suggested. "No one will be watching them or expecting them to go on the hunt for ring meanings."

Riley wanted to follow through on everything to do with the rings, Margaret's assignment and anything else tied to her connection with the Russian trinity knot rings.

"Toby needs you. If you start digging into the rings and their meaning, you might put him at risk again."

Charlie nodded. "Mack will be with you and the child until we're certain you aren't going to be taken again to be retrained and brainwashed. I'd feel better if you didn't go after the rings and their meanings."

"Me, too," Mack said.

Riley's mouth pressed into a thin line. "But it's my life. It's the reason all of this happened in the first place."

As if on cue, Toby entered the room with a tray

almost as big as he was, piled high with several different kinds of cookies. He was followed by the chef, who carried another tray with a large pitcher of lemonade and glasses filled with ice.

Riley took one look at the little boy's beaming face and knew she couldn't drag him into the fray again. Toby deserved a normal life where he wasn't being kidnapped or tortured by people who would use him as a spy in their own selfish or political machinations.

"Okay," Riley said quietly. "I'll leave it up to you to assign someone else to research the rings." She handed the rings back to Charlie and bent to Toby. "What have you got here?"

"Cookies," Toby said, a smile spreading across his face as he attempted to set the tray on a coffee table, nearly dumping the cookies on the floor.

Riley grabbed the tray on one side and Mack grabbed the other, steadying it until it rested solidly on the table.

"And Chef Saulnier has lemonade for everyone." He looked up at Riley. "May I have a cookie and lemonade with the big people?"

Riley smiled down at him. "Of course you may." She handed him a napkin. "Choose the one you want."

He reached for a large chocolate chip cookie and placed it on his napkin. "These are the best." He glanced at the chef. "No offense."

"None taken," the chef said, and backed out of the room, leaving them to enjoy the lemonade and cookies.

The men waited for Grace, Riley and Charlie to make their selections before they made their own.

Charlie held her cookie in her hand, her gaze slipping across each of the marines in her living room.

Riley could almost imagine the wheels turning in the older woman's mind. Finally, Charlie's gaze landed on one of the other men. "Mustang, how's the house hunting?"

He shrugged. "I'm still looking. I have a lease on an apartment that doesn't run out for another three months, so I have plenty of time to make a decision." He gave the widow a twisted smile. "Why do you ask?"

"I'm thinking, if you're not too busy house hunting, you might like to make a visit to this Russian expert."

He nodded. "I can do that. When would you like me to do this?"

"As soon as possible." Charlie crossed the room to him and laid the two rings in his palm as if placing the weight of the world in his hands. "I get the feeling these rings might give me a clue as to who murdered my husband."

Mustang closed his fingers around the rings. "I'll get right on it."

"Let me get a picture of those." Jonah pulled out his cell phone and snapped a photo of the rings in Mustang's palm. "I'll run a photo recognition on the rings as well."

"If you don't mind," Riley said, "I think it's about time to get Toby back home. He has a busy day ahead of him. He starts a new school tomorrow and I want him to be rested."

Mustang slipped the rings into his pocket and gave Mack a bear hug, clapping a hand against his back. "Glad we wrapped up this little party without losing any of us."

"Thank you all for your efforts in keeping me, Riley and Toby alive," Charlie said. "I couldn't have done it without Declan's Defenders. The marines don't know what they're missing, but I'm glad I found you. We might yet learn what happened to make someone want to kill my husband."

"We'll do the best we can. In the meantime, I wouldn't consider you out of danger," Declan said. "A kidnapping attempt and an order to poison you aren't leaving me feeling all warm and fuzzy."

Charlie drew in a deep breath and let it out slowly. "Thank goodness I have you all to look after me and others who come along. And thank you, Declan and Grace, for agreeing to move onto the estate until we resolve these issues."

Riley frowned. "You're moving out of the apartment?"

Grace nodded. "We haven't had time to talk, but yes. Since I'll be working closely with Charlie, she thought it would be best if I lived closer. And Declan will need easy access to the computer room and Jonah if he's going to lead the others in their work with Declan's Defenders."

"I'll miss you," Riley said.

"Yeah, but it will work out better, since you have Toby living with you now. You'll need that extra bedroom for him." Grace hugged Riley. "I'll move my things over the next week. Toby needs a room all his own."

Riley helped Toby clean up his cookie crumbles and wipe the chocolate off his face. Already, his eyes drooped, and he was ready to go home.

Mack lifted him in his arms, and the boy laid his cheek on the marine's shoulder.

Riley's heart swelled. The man would make a good father. Losing his own little brother at a young age had made him more aware of children and their needs.

Not only would he make a good father, he'd make a good husband. Not that she was thinking that far ahead. They'd only just met a week before. But she felt as if she'd known him much longer.

The man was honest, caring and protective. He'd be there for the ones he loved and give them what they needed.

Love.

Her pulse quickened as she contemplated the future. A future that included Mack and Toby.

"I can call a taxi to take us home. You don't have to drop us off," Riley offered, knowing she'd rather have Mack take them home. And when they got there, she'd ask him to come in for a drink and maybe more...

"I brought you here. I'll take you home." Mack frowned. "You're not trying to get rid of me, are you?"

She slipped her arm through the crook of his elbow. "On the contrary, I want to make sure you aren't getting tired of me and my ready-made family."

Mack patted Toby's back, a smile slipping across his face. "I kind of like this ready-made family. If you don't mind, I'd like to stick around. You know. Ask you on a date. With Toby, of course. We hardly got to know each other during all the excitement."

"I feel like I know you already." Riley leaned her cheek against his arm.

"I hope that's a good thing," he said.

"Only the best." She squeezed his arm and let go as they reached his truck and he opened the back door.

Mack settled Toby in the back seat and buckled him in. The boy's eyes never opened. He was down for the count, for the night.

Mack opened Riley's door.

She stepped into the opening without climbing up. Instead, she turned to face him.

He leaned in, closing the distance between them, and brushed his lips across hers. "I've wanted to do that all evening."

Riley wrapped her arms around his neck and stood on her toes to press her lips to his. "And I've wanted you to do that for the past four hours."

He settled his hands on her hips and pulled her close. "Does it matter that we haven't been on a first date?"

She shook her head. "Not in the least. I told you… I feel like I know you."

"You don't even know my favorite sports team or color or where I grew up."

She shook her head. "None of that matters. I know what's here." She pressed her hand to his chest. "You have a big heart, capable of a lot of love. That's all I need to know for now." She gripped his cheeks between her palms and angled his head down to hers and kissed him with all her heart and soul.

He held her against him, deepening the kiss until his tongue slipped past her teeth to caress hers in a long, sensual glide.

When at last they came up for air, Mack pressed his forehead against hers. "Always and forever," he murmured.

She leaned back and looked up into his eyes. "Why do you say that?"

"I think I could fall in love with you…always and forever."

Her heart felt as if it would burst. "Don't you think it's too soon to say that?"

He shook his head. "I know what's in my heart now. I'm not going to change my mind. But if you need more time to come to the same conclusion, I'll give it to you. I'm in this for the long haul."

"Good, because I can't think of anyone I'd rather spend my life getting to know." Riley looked up into the man's eyes, her own reflection shining back at her. "Always and forever."

* * * * *

Don't miss the next book in Elle James's
Declan's Defenders miniseries,
Available September 2019 wherever
Harlequin Intrigue books and ebooks are sold.

Jen Delaney loved Bent, Wyoming, the town she'd been born in,
grown up in. She was a respected member of the community, in
part because she ran the only store that sold groceries and other
essentials within a twenty-mile radius of town.

From her position crouched on the linoleum while she stocked
shelves, she looked around the small store she'd taken over at the
ripe age of eighteen. For the past ten years it had been her baby,
with its narrow aisles and hodgepodge of necessities.

She'd always known she'd spend the entirety of her life happily
ensconced in Bent and her store, no matter what happened around
her.

The reappearance of Ty Carson didn't change that knowledge
so much as make it…annoying. No, annoying would have been
just his being in town again. The fact their families had somehow
intermingled in the last year was…a catastrophe.

Her sister, Laurel, marrying Ty's cousin Grady had been a shock,
very close to a betrayal, though it was hard to hold it against Laurel
when Grady was so head over heels for her it was comical. They
both glowed with love and happiness and impending parenthood.

Jen tried not to hate them for it.

She could forgive Cam, her eldest brother, for his serious
relationship with Hilly. Hilly was biologically a Carson, but she'd
only just found that out. Besides, Hilly wasn't like other Carsons.
She was so sweet and earnest.

But Dylan and Vanessa… Her business-minded, sophisticated older brother *impregnating* and marrying snarky bad girl Vanessa Carson… *That* was a nightmare.

And none of it was fair. Jen was now, out of nowhere, surrounded by Carsons and Delaneys intermingling—which went against everything Bent had ever stood for. Carsons and Delaneys hated each other. They didn't fall in love and get married and have *babies*.

And still, she could have handled all that in a certain amount of stride if it weren't for *Ty* Carson. Everywhere she turned he seemed to be right there, his stoic gaze always locked on *her*, reminding her of a past she'd spent a lot of time trying to bury and forget.

When she'd been seventeen and the stupidest girl alive, she would have done anything for Ty Carson. Risked the Delaney-Carson curse that, even with all these Carson-Delaney marriages, Bent still had their heart set on. She would have risked her father's wrath over daring to connect herself with a *Carson*. She would have given up anything and everything for Ty.

Instead he'd made promises to love her forever, then disappeared to join the army—which she'd found out only a good month after the fact. He hadn't just broken her heart—he'd crushed it to bits.

But Ty was a blip of her past she'd been able to forget about, mostly, for the past ten years. She'd accepted his choices and moved on with her life. For a decade she had grown into the adult who didn't care at all about Ty Carson.

Then Ty had come home for good, and all she'd convinced herself of faded away.

She was half convinced he'd returned simply to make her miserable.

"You look angry. Must be thinking about me."

Don't miss
Wyoming Cowboy Ranger *by Nicole Helm,*
available June 2019 wherever
Harlequin® Intrigue books and ebooks are sold.

www.Harlequin.com

HIEXP0519

Dr. Rowan DuPont has returned to Winchester, Tennessee, to take over the family funeral home, but she is haunted by the memories of her family members' murders. Rowan is prepared to face her past in order to do right by her father's wishes...and to wait out his murderer, a serial killer who is obsessed with her.

Read on for a sneak preview of
The Secrets We Bury
by USA TODAY *bestselling author Debra Webb.*

Winchester, Tennessee
Monday, May 6, 7:15 a.m.

Mothers shouldn't die this close to Mother's Day.

Especially mothers whose daughters, despite being grown and having families of their own, still considered Mom to be their best friend. Rowan DuPont had spent the better part of last night consoling the daughters of Geneva Phillips. Geneva had failed to show at church on Sunday morning, and later that same afternoon she wasn't answering her cell. Her younger daughter entered her mother's home to check on her and found Geneva deceased in the bathtub.

Now the seventy-two-year-old woman's body waited in refrigeration for Rowan to begin the preparations for her final journey. The viewing wasn't until tomorrow evening, so there was no particular rush. The husband of one of the daughters was away on business in London and wouldn't arrive back home until late today. There was time for a short break, which turned into a morning drive that had taken Rowan across town and to a place she hadn't visited in more than two decades.

Like death, some things were inevitable. Coming back to this place was one of those things. Perhaps it was the hours spent with the sisters last night that had prompted memories of Rowan's own sister. She and her twin had once been inseparable. Wasn't that generally the way with identical twins?

The breeze shifted, lifting a wisp of hair across her face. Rowan swiped it away and stared out over Tims Ford Lake. The dark, murky waters spread like sprawling arms some thirty-odd miles upstream from the nearby dam, enveloping the treacherous Elk River in its embrace. The water was deep and unforgiving. Even standing on the bank, at least ten feet from the edge, a chill crept up Rowan's spine. She hated this place. Hated the water. The ripples that broke the shadowy surface…the smell of fish and rotting plant life. She hated every little thing about it.

This was the spot where her sister's body had been found.

Don't miss
The Secrets We Bury *by Debra Webb,*
available May 2019 wherever
MIRA® books and ebooks are sold.

www.Harlequin.com

  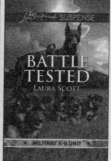
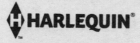

Love Harlequin romance?

DISCOVER.

Be the first to find out about promotions, news and exclusive content!

Facebook.com/HarlequinBooks

Twitter.com/HarlequinBooks

Instagram.com/HarlequinBooks

Pinterest.com/HarlequinBooks

ReaderService.com

EXPLORE.

Sign up for the Harlequin e-newsletter and download a free book from any series at **TryHarlequin.com.**

CONNECT.

Join our Harlequin community to share your thoughts and connect with other romance readers!
Facebook.com/groups/HarlequinConnection

HARLEQUIN®

ROMANCE WHEN YOU NEED IT

HSOCIAL2018